"If you're in danger, I can help."

Your presence puts me in danger. "I'm fine. I just want to get back to a normal life with my Kaitlyn." Her daughter had to be her total focus.

"Juanita is missing."

The very thought scared her even more than she already was. That could be her, her daughter or her uncle. If she said anything.

The drill of his gaze bore through her. For a few seconds she wanted to tell him everything. But the intruder's threat replayed through her mind and the words stuck in her throat.

She needed to get out of here. How did she think she could have a conversation with the Texas Ranger and leave unscathed?

Books by Margaret Daley

MARGARET DALEY

feels she has been blessed. She has been married more than thirty years to her husband, Mike, whom she met in college. He is a terrific support and her best friend. They have one son, Shaun. Margaret has been writing for many years and loves to tell a story. When she was a little girl, she would play with her dolls and make up stories about their lives. Now she writes these stories down. She especially enjoys weaving stories about families and how faith in God can sustain a person when things get tough. When she isn't writing, she is fortunate to be a teacher for students with special needs. Margaret has taught for more than twenty years and loves working with her students. She has also been a Special Olympics coach and has participated in many sports with her students.

MARGARET DALEY

TRAIL OF LIES

Love Inspired

Special thanks and acknowledgment to Margaret Daley for her contribution to the Texas Ranger Justice miniseries.

Recycling programs for this product may not exist in your area.

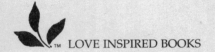

LOVE INSPIRED BOOKS

ISBN-13: 978-0-373-67458-9

TRAIL OF LIES

www.LoveInspiredBooks.com

Printed in U.S.A.

Casting all your care upon Him;
for He careth for you.
—1 *Peter* 5:7

To Terri Reed, Lenora Worth, Valerie Hansen
Lynette Eason and Shirlee McCoy—
it was great working with you all.

To all the Texas Rangers in the present day and the past.

ONE

Melora Hudson punched in her alarm code to turn the security system off, then tossed her keys on the kitchen counter. All she wanted to do was sink into a chair and drink a cup of hot tea after her exhausting week. But as she moved toward the kettle on the stove, a sound—something hitting the tiled floor—came from the living room and froze her in mid-stride. Tension whipped through her. Until her cat shot through the doorway and launched himself into her arms.

"Okay, Patches, what have you gotten into this time?"

His cry—like a baby's—protested her scolding.

Melora cuddled the fifteen-pound white cat against her chest and started for the living room. Just what she needed—another broken lamp or, like the last time, a crystal vase. As she approached the entrance, she mentally prepared for the devastation, realizing she could never get rid of the animal because her daughter loved Patches. And so did she.

A few steps into the room, Melora stopped, scanning the large expanse for any sign of what had made the crashing noise.

The desk chair was overturned at the far end. Strange. How had Patches done that? She placed the large cat on the tiled floor and headed across the room. Nothing he did should surprise her anymore. She began to pick up the chair while Patches weaved in and out of her legs, but stopped. Her nape prickled; unease streaked down her spine. The quiet of the house, usually a balm, was now ominous. She glanced toward the study.

She wasn't alone.

That thought bolted her to the floor for a few precious seconds before she whirled and ran toward the back porch off the great room. Halfway to the exit, she noticed the lock wasn't turned right.

The door was unlocked. Alarm squeezed her chest.

She peered sideways and spied a wiry, medium-sized man wearing a black ski mask barreling toward her. Pushing herself faster, she reached for the knob. Two feet away.

He tackled her. The impact of the cool tiles knocked the breath from her, pain radiating through her. His body trapped her beneath him.

All the fear from that break-in two years ago came to the foreground.

She twisted and bucked, trying to shove him off her. She drew in a gulp of air. Finally, her protest ripped from her throat and ricocheted off the tall ceilings, filling the room with her terror.

He slapped her across the face. "Shut up."

Texas Ranger Daniel Boone Riley turned his white Ford 150 truck down the road that led to the Hudson's house in Lone Star Estates where many wealthy San Antonians lived. He should know. His family mansion wasn't but a mile from here.

He'd seen Melora Hudson, the widow, at her husband's funeral a couple of days before. A picture of a five-foot, six-inch, willowy woman materialized in his mind. While she'd stood at the gravesite, her red hair with golden highlights had caught the sun's rays, accentuating the long curls about her beautiful face—a solemn face, appropriate for a funeral. Until he'd locked gazes with her for a few seconds and something akin to fear had flashed into her sea-green eyes. She'd immediately looked away, but he'd seen the apprehension.

What did she know about her husband's death? What was she hiding?

He was here to find out. He'd spent the last few days learning everything he could about the woman. Although Axle Hudson had been murdered two years ago and his body only found last month and not identified until the previous week, the man's death was tied to the recent murder of Captain Gregory Pike of the Texas Rangers' Company D. Daniel would stop at nothing to discover that link. Gregory had been a good friend as well as his boss. There was no way any Ranger in Company D would allow his murder to go unsolved—even though few leads had been uncovered in the month since Greg's death. They knew his murder was connected to an elusive group of people called the Lions of Texas who dealt in illegal activities—drugs among them. Had Axle Hudson been involved in drug dealing? One of many questions Daniel wanted answered.

He parked his truck in front of the large, Spanish-style house with stucco accents and a tile roof. It fit into its surroundings and shouted wealth—typical of what he'd known of Axle Hudson, a flamboyant playboy who had finally married Melora Madison, the niece of prominent businessman Tyler Madison, in a wedding that had been the event of the social season in San Antonio six years ago.

As he strode toward the porch, a scream rent the air. A woman's scream coming from the house. He pulled his Wilson Combat pistol from his waist holster and rushed toward the porch. When he tried the handle, the door was locked. He took a few steps back, started to lift his leg to kick the heavy solid door and realized he wouldn't be able to budge it.

Daniel needed an entrance into the house other than the sturdy front door. Swiveling to the right, he jogged toward the side, placing a call to the sheriff for back up. He found a flimsier door next to the three-car garage and put all his strength behind kicking in the wooden structure. It exploded inward, and he burst into the mudroom.

The pressure on Melora's chest caused dots to dance before her eyes. Sweat coated her face, her body.

Her attacker's dark gaze trailed down her, leaving her chilled. With her arms pinned to her side and the man's heavy weight on her, fear drenched her like her perspiration.

"I won't hurt you if you keep quiet." The raspy voice, as if he'd smoked one too many cigarettes, didn't give his words a ring of truth.

His smelly odor assailed her. Nausea roiled in her stomach. "What do you want?" she managed to squeak out, so glad her daughter was playing at a friend's. If Kaitlyn had been here… The thought chilled her blood.

The intruder withdrew a switchblade and flicked it open. "Information. It was about time you got home."

Melora's eyes grew round, focused totally on the

knife he held before her. Not far from her heart. Her throat.

"Where's the flash drive your husband always had on him?"

"I don't know." The flash drive Axle wore around his neck? What had he done to cause this continual nightmare?

The blade came closer. "There are two dumb things you can do. Not give me the flash drive and talk to the police about this or anything concerning your husband's affairs. Are you smart? I'd hate your little girl to be without a mommy. Where's the flash drive? It wasn't found with your husband's body. It has to be here."

The gleaming metal commanded her full attention. Until a boom rocked the air. It sounded as though something had slammed against the wall.

The intruder jerked up, his focus on the entrance into the living room.

Melora grabbed the split second of distraction and shoved upward with all her strength. The man, taken by surprise, teetered above her, the knife clanging to the floor.

Totally in cop mode with his gun clasped in his hand, Daniel quickly assessed the kitchen and moved toward the hallway. A noise to his right— like a scuffle—drew him into the living room. On the far side, a man with a ski mask leaped to his feet and spun around.

"Halt! State Police," Daniel shouted, aiming his gun.

Out of the corner of his eye, he glimpsed Melora sprawled on the floor, her eyes huge in her pale face, a knife a few feet from her on the floor. She scrambled back from her attacker.

As though he had nothing to lose, the intruder sprang for the porch door, wrenched it open, then plunged through the opening.

As Daniel raced toward the exit after the man, he glanced at Melora. "Are you okay?"

"Yes." Her answer came out with a shaky rasp, her face leached of all color.

"I called the sheriff. Help is on the way."

He hurried after the attacker who swung over the railing and landed in the grass below, then shot toward the side of the house. Daniel took the same route. The second his feet touched the ground, he sprinted forward, rounding the pool and cabana not far behind the assailant.

When the man scaled the fence separating the Hudson's property from the neighbor's, his foot caught on a wooden railing, and he tumbled over. Daniel pushed himself faster, eating up several yards between them before the intruder hustled to his feet and continued toward a vehicle parked on the street.

Daniel sailed over the same fence, adrenaline spurring him on. Determined to catch the burglar, he raced across the neighbor's front lawn. When the assailant reached a white Honda Accord, he dragged the door open and lunged inside.

The car started, and the intruder floored the gas, shrieking away from the curb. Daniel zeroed in on the license plate and got a partial number, the rest obscured by dirt. He lifted his gun to aim at the back left tire, knowing the possibility of stopping the car was slim.

Too late. The vehicle disappeared around the corner.

Daniel dug into his pocket and withdrew his cell, calling the suspect's car and partial plate number into the sheriff's office. Then he trudged back to the Hudson's house, which sat on several acres of land. The picture of Melora on the floor, afraid, her shirt pulled out of her slacks, her long hair tousled, her body quaking, haunted his thoughts. The visualization rocked him with anger.

What was going on? That question plagued him the whole way back as he retraced his steps to see if the suspect had dropped anything in his mad dash to get away. Nothing.

Climbing the steps to the deck, Daniel holstered his pistol. When he entered the living room, he discovered Melora standing not far from where she'd been attacked. Her shirt was tucked into her pants, and she was running her trembling hand through her hair. The pale cast to her face, and the large, round eyes spoke of a woman who had been frightened for her life.

He needed answers, ones his fellow Ranger Oliver Drew hadn't gotten when he had interviewed her last week after Axle Hudson's remains had finally been identified. "Did this have anything to do with your husband's murder?" Daniel covered the short distance between them.

She backed up, her arms crossing her chest. "I think…" Her tongue ran over her lips. "I think it was just a burglar."

He couldn't shake the feeling something was going on here beyond a mere robbery, especially since Melora kept evading eye contact. "What was he after?"

Her mouth pinched into a frown. "I don't know. He didn't give me a rundown while he had me pinned to the floor."

Her body language—rubbing her eye, looking away for a couple of seconds—shouted at deception. She knew what the man was after. Why didn't she tell him? Was there a connection to her dead husband?

"You're Daniel Riley with the Texas Rangers. I told the other Ranger last week I don't know who would have killed my husband or why someone would want him dead. Why would you think this has anything to do with Axle's murder?" She drew herself up straight, dropping her arms to her sides, her chin tilting up a notch.

They had casually met before since their families moved in the same social circles, and she was on the Alamo Planning Committee for the 175th anniversary celebration of the Battle of the Alamo in March. He'd spoken to the committee a few months back. But he really didn't know her. That would change after today. "Why are you so sure it doesn't? Your husband's remains were finally identified after he'd been missing for two years and the next week your house is broken into. Just a coincidence?"

"Yes. I've told Ranger Drew everything I know, which is nothing. Axle went out one evening and never returned. That's all I know."

"Did anyone have a grudge against your husband?"

"Why are the Texas Rangers involved in the investigation? I would have thought the sheriff would be conducting the murder investigation. He's the one I reported to when my husband went missing two years ago."

"Your husband's murder may be tied to an investigation we're running."

"What?"

The doorbell's chime cut the tension vibrating between them.

"Excuse me." Relief washed over her face as she headed toward the foyer.

"That's the sheriff. I called in the make of the getaway car and its partial license number." Daniel trailed behind her, just in case it wasn't the sheriff.

She halted and looked back at him. "Good."

But that fear he'd glimpsed at the gravesite flickered across her face momentarily. She quickly continued her trek toward the door and opened it to the sheriff and a deputy.

Sheriff Karl Layton moved into the house after indicating to his deputy to check the grounds. "Melora, I understand there was a break-in here today."

"A man was here when I came home a little while ago."

"Where are your housekeeper and daughter?"

"Juanita took Kaitlyn to a play date with a friend. I had a meeting at the hospital with the ladies auxiliary."

"When will they be back?"

"Not for another hour."

"I'll try to make this quick. I'd hate to upset Kaitlyn any more."

"Thanks, Karl. I appreciate that." Melora indicated to the living room and Daniel standing in its entrance. "Ranger Riley managed to thwart the man. Nothing was taken that I can tell."

How would she know? She couldn't have checked. There hadn't been enough time. Daniel got the distinct feeling the woman wanted both him and the sheriff gone as quickly as possible. That wasn't going to happen. She wasn't getting rid of him that easily. Her husband had been involved in what was going on with the Lions of Texas. His body had been found buried at one of the organization's drug drop sites. Had he been a member of the group? Had he crossed them somehow? Did Melora know something about the Lions of Texas?

Daniel strode to where the knife lay on the floor and pointed at it. "The intruder dropped this before fleeing."

The color that had returned to Melora's face drained again as she looked at the weapon. She turned away, hugging her arms across her chest.

"Good. We'll check for fingerprints." The sheriff donned a latex glove and carefully picked up the knife to drop into an evidence bag.

"You probably won't find anything since he wore gloves, but maybe he was careless and we'll catch a break."

"It's happened before, and I'm always grateful when it does." Karl removed his cowboy hat and held it in his hands as he sat on a beige couch while Melora took the wingback chair across from him.

"Can you tell me what happened? Anything about the man?"

She ran her long tapered fingers along her chin. "It happened so fast. I thought Patches had knocked over something in the living room. I came in to investigate. The next thing I know a man tackled me to the floor. The rest is a blur."

Daniel remained standing by the door to the porch, listening to the shaky thread in her voice. His instincts told him there was a lot more to the story.

"What did he look like?" The sheriff rotated his cowboy hat in his hands.

"He had a black ski mask on. That's about all I really saw."

"What color were his eyes?" Daniel asked as he took several steps toward the pair.

"I—green—no, I think brown." Melora kept her gaze fastened on to the sheriff as though hoping Daniel would go away if she ignored him.

Frustration churned in his gut. "Sheriff Layton, the suspect was about five feet nine. His build was compact. Strands of black hair hung below the ski mask a few inches. He was wearing dark blue jeans and a gray T-shirt, plain as far as I could tell and black leather gloves. His arms were deeply tanned. I gave you the description of the car he used to get away. Oh, and he ran fast, as though he were a runner."

"That's a start. We've got a BOLO out on the car."

"Will you let me know when you find it?" Although he knew the sheriff would follow up on the partial license plate and see if he could find a match with a white Honda Accord, Daniel planned to do his own checking into it. He had to do something to find the person who murdered his captain. So much of what he and the other Rangers of Company D had discovered had led nowhere. They knew there was a criminal group in the state called the Lions of Texas and two of the activities they were involved in were drug running and murder. Axle had obviously doublecrossed them, and he paid the price. His body was a clue Daniel hoped steered them in the right direction.

"Sure." The sheriff turned his attention back to Melora. "Do you have any idea how the suspect got into the house?"

She waved her hand toward the porch door. "It was unlocked. The bolt was in the wrong place. I know it was locked when I left and my alarm was on when I came home."

"Who knows your alarm code?" the sheriff asked, removing a pad from his pocket.

"My housekeeper, a maid who comes twice a week to clean and my uncle." She rubbed her temple. "I think that's all. I don't make it a habit to give out my code."

"Who's the maid?" The sheriff jotted something down.

"Alicia Wells, but she's been with me for years. The same with Juanita. She worked for my uncle before she came to me when I got married. I don't see either one involved in robbing me."

While Melora gave the sheriff Alicia's address, Daniel strode to the porch door and checked it out.

"It doesn't look like the lock has been tampered with. Who has a key to this door?" Daniel moved back toward Melora.

"The same people. The same key fits all my doors. But again, I can't see Alicia or Juanita trying to rob me. And my uncle certainly wouldn't."

Daniel knew her uncle. Tyler Madison was part of the same social circle as his parents. Although now that his father had died, Daniel's mother didn't go out much. "Where does Juanita live?"

"Here. She has a suite and has lived here since the beginning of my marriage. She's like family." Melora narrowed her eyes on Daniel, daring him to say otherwise.

The sheriff rose, sympathy on his face. "I'll talk with Alicia Wells and come back later to see if Juanita knows anything. I don't have to tell you to change your locks and code."

"I'll interview Juanita, Sheriff, and let you know what she says."

The sheriff nodded toward Daniel. "Fine. I'll leave my deputy to finish processing the scene. Melora, if you find anything missing or remember anything, call me. I'll have some deputies cruise by here and keep an eye on the place."

In one fluid motion she was on her feet, but Daniel noticed her hands still trembled. She clasped them together and walked the sheriff to the door. Daniel scanned the room, looking for anything out of place. Other than the desk chair knocked over, everything seemed as though it were in its place. So if it was a burglar, why didn't he see any evidence that the man was searching for valuables? Had she interrupted him right after he'd broken into the house? And why did he bother to reset the alarm if it was just a burglary? Most thieves get in and out fast. Was he waiting for Melora to come home and didn't want to alert her to his presence?

When she reentered the room, she drew in a deep breath. She wasn't a very good actress. Relief that the sheriff was gone was visible in her expression and the way she carried herself. But the second she spied him, her full tension returned. She stuffed her hands into the front pockets of her expensive brown slacks.

"Who is Patches?" Daniel finally took a seat in a chair.

She stared at him a few, long seconds before she

covered the distance and sat where the sheriff had. "He's my cat."

"Where is he?"

"He hides when strangers are here. Now that I think about how he flew into my arms, I should have known something was wrong."

"How do you really know the man didn't take anything?"

She blinked, her eyes large for a brief moment, then her expression neutralized. "I didn't see him carrying anything with him. Did you?" One eyebrow rose as though challenging him.

"There are items that are small but valuable. Jewelry, for one. I would suggest you confirm nothing was taken. I'll go with you to make sure the house is secure. Then I'll wait for Juanita to return."

She gripped the edges of the couch cushion. "Let me get something straight with you. Juanita didn't have anything to do with this. Over the years, she's had plenty of opportunities to rob me."

"I still want to talk with her. Your daughter and housekeeper should be home by the time we finish checking the house and you call a locksmith to come out here to change your locks."

"I can go through everything later."

"I'm here to help you. You do want to find the man who attacked you?"

Melora sat up straight, her mouth firmed in a

frown. "Of course, but I don't want Kaitlyn to know about any of this. She's only five and with all that's happened lately she's understandably upset."

"Then, when she comes home, just introduce me as a friend who's visiting." He stood. "We probably should get moving if we want to be finished before they arrive. I'll see what I can do about the door I kicked in. I wouldn't want your daughter to see it and get upset."

Her teeth dug into her lower lip as her eyelids closed. "Yes." But she didn't move for a long moment.

When she pushed to her feet and her gaze met his, for a few seconds he glimpsed fear in the depths of her green eyes. Weariness lined her beautiful features, triggering his concern. "I'm here to help you. You can trust me."

Daniel's words replayed through Melora's mind as she called a locksmith and a handyman she'd used before to replace the door and locks and as she and the Texas Ranger worked their way through the house. She didn't know the meaning of the word trust anymore. With the discovery of her husband's body, the nightmare that had started two years ago with his disappearance was back to plague her.

For almost two years, she'd managed to live

her life as if everything was normal. But it had never really been normal since she'd married Axle Hudson six years ago. She'd become trapped in a marriage to a man who had criminal connections and a cruel streak. Not even her uncle could have helped her. Axle had been like a son to him and her husband could do no wrong in his eyes. How would Uncle Tyler ever believe Axle was a criminal, especially when she had no proof?

Even she'd had a hard time believing Axle's chain of restaurants might be a front for illegal activities. Not the man she'd loved. But once he'd caught her eavesdropping on one of his conversations while she tried to figure out what was going on. After that, the atmosphere in the house had changed. His subtle comments about the value of life and how he would hate for their daughter not to have a mother scared her so much. To the point that she'd started planning her escape from him.

Then Axle went missing. And if she'd still believed in God, she would have thought He'd stepped in and taken care of her problem. That all changed, however, when her house was trashed and she was threatened by two unknown men only days after she'd reported her husband's disappearance to the authorities.

Keep quiet and stay put and you won't end up like your husband—dead. The intruders' words two years ago flashed in and out of her mind.

They'd been after Axle's flash drive then, too. She stumbled as she returned to the living room.

Daniel grasped her arm and steadied her. The brand of his fingers around her biceps zipped a fiery path through her.

She stepped away, needing space. "I told you the man didn't take anything. My jewelry is all there. Even my husband's coin collection is intact. And it's quite valuable."

"Still, it needed to be checked out. You must have interrupted him right after he came. Not much was even disturbed except in the office. Do you use that room much?"

"No." She shivered. That had been her husband's domain and the place where he had threatened her if she continued to snoop into his activities. After that, she'd avoided his office. "Other than a few important pieces of paper my uncle needed concerning the restaurant chain, I've left it as is." She had been so grateful that her uncle had seen to Axle's business. She'd wanted to sell it and distance herself as far as possible from what could be an illegal enterprise, but because her husband wasn't dead, only missing, she couldn't do anything. But that all changed last week when his body was identified after being found buried on a local animal rescue's property.

"Your uncle? Tyler Madison? What does he have to do with your husband's restaurant chain?"

"When Axle wasn't found, I took over the temporary running of the business. My uncle was the one who helped me and found a top-notch man to run it until Axle turned up." She stared at the door her attacker had disappeared through only an hour before. "I'm afraid business isn't my forte. I needed someone who was an expert. Uncle Tyler had the perfect man."

"Ah, so you don't know much about your husband's business?"

She shook her head. Axle had purposefully kept her in the dark about his dealings and finances. "Eating at the restaurants is the extent of my knowledge concerning them. But the business is part of Axle's estate and my daughter's legacy." And she had every intention of selling the chain as soon as she could. She didn't want her daughter connected in any way to something illegal. With the Texas Rangers suddenly interested in Axle's business, all her fears that the restaurant chain was somehow tied to criminal activities were validated.

Daniel gestured toward the couch. "What does Axle's will say? Who stands to gain from your husband's murder?"

"My daughter, who is five years old. Everything was left to her in a trust. I have a yearly allowance and this house."

"Did you know the terms of the will before your husband's death?"

"Yes. But my uncle has provided for me in his will. Besides, I also have the trust my parents set up for me. I didn't need Axle's money." Her only goal was to look out for her daughter and her well-being. Although exhaustion clung to her, she remained standing in spite of Daniel taking a seat. "Are you accusing me of killing my husband?"

"No, should I?"

TWO

Melora collapsed into the chair near her. The thought that someone would suspect she could have something to do with a murder stunned her. "I was surrounded by people in the days around my husband's disappearance. My housekeeper who lives here. My uncle stayed with me when Axle didn't come home and I couldn't get in touch with him. The day he disappeared I was at a conference in Dallas. My daughter was here with Juanita, and when Axle didn't come home, I had her go to my uncle's until I could get back to San Antonio."

"I just like covering all the facts and details of a case. I've been assigned to find out what happened to your husband."

"Again, I want to know what case you're working on."

"One that could have far-reaching consequences. That's all I can tell you right now."

And she wouldn't tell him that she had contacted the FBI in Dallas after her conference to tell them the little she knew about her husband's activities. Axle had let her go to the conference since she was the chairperson of the committee working for the mayor on drug education. He'd known she wouldn't do anything with Kaitlyn in his hands, that she would never leave her daughter behind in San Antonio. But also, she was sure Axle had her followed. That feeling had stayed with her during her brief time in Dallas and all the way back to San Antonio. She still felt she was being watched. All she wanted was for Daniel Riley to leave her and her daughter alone.

She massaged her temples. "I don't know anything more and my daughter will be home any minute. I don't want anyone upsetting her." She pointedly stabbed him with her gaze. The door he'd used to come into the house was through the mudroom, which she could close off so Kaitlyn wouldn't see the busted door.

"I'd like to talk with Juanita, but I'll make sure Kaitlyn doesn't know why I'm here."

"I appreciate that. She doesn't understand why her daddy was gone for so long and then last week we had a funeral for him." The sound of the garage door going up rumbled through the house. Melora wearily shoved herself to her feet. "Juanita and Kaitlyn are home."

He followed her into the kitchen. "I noticed your daughter was at the funeral."

Yes, and Melora had noticed he had been there, too, with the other Texas Ranger, Anderson Michaels, who'd come to the Alamo Planning Committee in October. Another committee she was on. Axle had wanted her to project the right image to the world, and she'd never complained because she liked making a difference and helping where she could. In fact, she still tried to maintain as normal a schedule as possible although she'd buried her husband two days ago.

She threw him a glance. "Kaitlyn needed some closure with her father." She hoped instead of Kaitlyn getting distressed because her father hadn't come home that her daughter's nightmares would stop since she'd gotten to say goodbye to her daddy at the funeral.

The knob on the door to the garage turned. Melora fortified herself with a deep breath and faced her daughter who raced into the room with Juanita trailing at a more sedate pace.

"Mommy, you're home." Kaitlyn threw her arms around Melora's legs. "I had a great time at Cara's."

While her housekeeper made her way toward her suite off a back hallway, Melora hugged Kaitlyn. "I'm so glad. We'll have to have Cara over here soon."

"Tomorrow?" Her daughter bent back and looked up expectedly.

Melora forced a chuckle that fell flat. "We'll see."

Kaitlyn leaned around Melora, peering at Daniel Riley. "Who are you?"

He crossed the kitchen, a smile lighting his gray eyes as though they were pieces of silver. "I'm a friend of your mother's."

Her daughter tilted her head and studied the Texas Ranger. "How come I've never seen you?"

His shoulders lifted in a shrug. "That's going to change today. I'm Daniel."

She tapped her chest. "I'm Kaitlyn."

"I thought so. Your mother talks about you a lot."

Kaitlyn beamed. "Yeah, she tells me all the time I'm her pride and joy."

"I can see why."

"Have ya met Patches yet?"

"No, I haven't."

"He's hiding. He does that all the time with someone new." Kaitlyn stepped closer and lowered her voice. "Don't worry. He'll get used to you. Then he won't leave you alone."

Melora moved forward to break up the little bonding session. She wanted the Texas Ranger out of her house as soon as possible. "Speaking of Patches, aren't you supposed to feed him, young lady?"

"Yeah." Kaitlyn turned her full attention back to

Daniel. "Would ya like to help? I'll hold Patches while you pat him."

"Hon, he needs to leave."

Daniel shot Melora a look that said their conversation wasn't over. "Yeah, I'm sorry I have to go. But I'm sure I'll see you again, Kaitlyn."

"Great! I'll show you Patches then." Her child hurried toward the utility room where Patches's food was kept.

Once Kaitlyn was out of the kitchen, Daniel said, "I'd like to talk to Juanita before I leave."

Melora peered toward where her daughter had disappeared. She needed to get rid of the man as fast as possible in case someone was watching the house. "Fine. I'll take you back to her suite. After that, I'd like you to go. I don't want Kaitlyn to know anything about today."

"Don't you want to find out who murdered your husband? Who broke into your house? It's possible there's a connection."

While he studied her, she struggled to remain as calm as possible. "Of course. But I don't see a connection. And I have to think of my daughter's emotional well-being." *And her physical well-being.* What if Kaitlyn had been here when the man had broken in? Both sets of intruders had frightened her, but the last one seemed more sinister—desperate almost, as though time was running out. Chills encased her in a cold sweat. Her heartbeat sped up. She didn't know how long she could keep up the pretense that everything was all right. This facade she had to put on weighed heavily on her.

"I shouldn't be long."

Melora swept her arm across her front, indicating the hallway Juanita disappeared down, then started forward. "Her room is back here."

The hair on her nape tingled under the Ranger's hard gaze. He wasn't going to let this investigation die until he'd turned over every clue he could get. Fear mingled with her frustration. She hadn't wanted to say anything to Uncle Tyler about what had happened two years ago. She didn't want him worrying or worse—trying to do something about it and getting hurt. He'd taken her in after her parents died when she was nine. He was all the family she had except for Kaitlyn.

Melora stopped in front of a closed door and knocked. Her housekeeper answered, peering first at her then Daniel, wariness in her dark eyes. Although she knew about the break-in after Axle had vanished, Melora hadn't told her about the threat. And Juanita had never questioned why Melora hadn't reported the break-in to the sheriff. Juanita was an American citizen, but she was leery of law enforcement. Some of her family had been deported back to Mexico.

"This is Daniel Riley with the Texas Rangers. He has a few questions for you. We had an intruder today, and Ranger Riley managed to chase the man away but didn't catch him."

Juanita's attention remained focused on Melora for a few seconds. "I don't know anything about a break-in."

Touching her arm, Melora gave her housekeeper a reassuring look. "I know." She bit back the words, "Humor him and he'll leave."

"May I come in?" Daniel asked, nodding toward the sitting area visible behind Juanita.

"I was getting ready to leave. I have to get dinner ready." The housekeeper blocked the entrance into her suite. "I don't understand what you think I know. I wasn't here." She shifted her gaze to Melora. "Was anything taken? Nothing was bothered in my room."

"No, not that I can tell."

"Who left first, you or Mrs. Hudson this afternoon?" Daniel asked, scrutinizing the housekeeper.

"I did with Kaitlyn. I had a few errands to run before the play date."

"What errands?"

"Pharmacy and dry cleaners." Juanita glanced at Melora.

"Did you talk to anyone?" Daniel shifted to hamper Juanita's view of Melora.

"Just the cashiers."

"Did you notice a white Honda Accord parked in this area when you left?"

Juanita tilted her head to the side and thought for a moment. "No."

"No one unusual around?"

Juanita shook her head.

Daniel withdrew a business card. "If you can think of anything that might help us find the man who broke in here, please contact me."

Pocketing the card, her housekeeper moved out into the hall and closed her door. "If that's all, I've got dinner to cook." She ambled toward the kitchen without giving Daniel a chance to say anything.

"She's tough," Daniel said with a chuckle.

"Yes, and observant, so if she said she didn't see anyone, there wasn't anyone out there."

"What time did you leave this afternoon?"

"1:00. My meeting was at 2:00 and since we're a ways out of San Antonio, I needed to leave early. And I didn't see anyone, either." She trailed after her housekeeper down the hall, again feeling the Ranger's scrutiny.

"Either the man is good at hiding or he came after you left. Do you follow a certain routine?"

"No. This meeting, however, is public knowledge and so is my participation." Remembering that the man had indicated he'd been waiting for her return made her fearful. Her hands quavered, and she had to curl them into fists to keep the Ranger from seeing her alarm.

"But the man wouldn't know about your daughter and her play date?"

The question brought Melora up short. She gripped the frame of the door that led into the kitchen. "So you think he either didn't care my daughter would be home or he was watching the place?"

Daniel skirted around her. "It's a possibility we need to consider." The pounding of her heartbeat nearly drowned out his next words, "I'll keep you informed of my investigation."

In other words, he'd keep in touch, possibly come back to the house. Alert whoever was watching her. She wanted to tell him she didn't want the case pursued, but there was no way she could tell him her reasons. She didn't know what to do anymore.

Why, Axle? Why did you get mixed up in something illegal? Those questions had rumbled around in her mind for the past two years, and she was reminded yet again that her judgment concerning her husband hadn't been good. What had she missed? Why couldn't she have seen what kind of man he really was?

"Mrs. Hudson?"

Daniel's voice, full of concern, wrenched her

back to the present—a present filled with a Texas Ranger who asked too many questions.

"Are you okay?"

She blinked. "What do you think?"

He peered over her shoulder at the housekeeper and moved close to her. "I think you're scared and hiding something." He tipped his cowboy hat. "Good day. I can find my own way out."

Melora watched the man stride away, his steps long, economical, as though he never had a wasted motion. Dressed in tan slacks and a white, long-sleeve shirt with a black tie, he looked the part of a Texas Ranger down to his brown boots, his white cowboy hat and silver star he wore over his heart. Confident. Controlled. Capable—in any situation.

She wished she had those traits, especially right now. Then she would know who to trust, what to do. How to get out of the mess her husband had put her and Kaitlyn in.

Frustration churned Daniel's gut. Everywhere he'd gone he'd run into dead ends. But he knew that Axle's widow wasn't telling him everything. Behind the exhaustion, he glimpsed fear. Of what? He intended to find out. Somehow he felt it was connected to her husband's murder and possibly Captain Pike's. It wasn't just the break-in that had scared her.

Daniel could still remember the text message he'd received, along with all the Texas Rangers in Company D, from Captain Pike three months ago. His last one. *Convene at my house, ASAP. Major case about to explode.* When they'd arrived, they found him dead from a gunshot wound and another man critically injured. That man still hadn't woken up or been identified. If only one of the Rangers had gotten there before someone had killed their captain.

Daniel pulled into the parking lot of the Texas Ranger's station in San Antonio. On the way here from Melora's house, he'd had Ranger Oliver Drew run the partial license plate numbers against white Honda Accords in Texas. He hoped the list wasn't too long. He needed a break. After climbing from his truck, he strode toward the building, the temperature warmer than usual for the end of November, a hint of rain in the air.

Inside he found Oliver right away, sitting at his desk. "Did you get anything?"

"A list of seven vehicles in the San Antonio area—more for the whole state of Texas."

"Seven. That's not bad. First check them and see if there are any that have been reported stolen. Maybe the suspect was dumb enough to use his own car."

Oliver chuckled. "You're dreaming, but I'll take care of this list for you. Captain wants to see you."

Daniel looked toward Captain Benjamin Fritz's office. As a lieutenant, Daniel often ran things by his captain. Pushing open Ben's door, he stuck his head in. "You wanted to see me?"

"Yep, come in. I need you and Anderson to go back to the Alamo Planning Committee meeting. I don't like what's been happening. A lot of important dignitaries will be attending the celebration. Stress that, with the threatening letter the committee received in October and the phone call Hank Zarvy got a few weeks ago about the event, we want them to think about having a smaller, more intimate event for the 175th anniversary of the Battle of the Alamo. We think it would be better and far safer. I know the threats have been vague. Nothing but warnings that if we don't cancel the celebration, something bad will happen. But we haven't been able to trace anything."

"Okay. I'll check when the next meeting is and get on the agenda." Daniel immediately thought of the last meeting he'd gone to. Melora was on the committee. Maybe he could talk to her afterward. In a different environment after she had time to think about the break-in, she might be more forthcoming with her information.

"How did it go with Mrs. Hudson?"

"She's not saying much." He went on to give Ben a detailed report of the break-in and his interview with Melora and Juanita.

"Get Gisella to help you with digging into Axle Hudson's background and dealings. We need to know everything about him."

"Especially if he's a member of the Lions of Texas. You can certainly say he was a powerful person with lots of connections." One of the first breaks in their captain's murder case was the few details about the group they got from Eddie Jimenez, a low-level member of the Lions of Texas, who had tried to get the captain's notes after the shooting. Eddie hadn't been successful in getting what he had been after. When caught, the thug hadn't been able to tell them who had killed Gregory Pike or who had sent Eddie after the notes, but the man did tell the Rangers that the group behind all this was called the Lions of Texas. According to Eddie the members were powerful—and very dangerous. Not much to go on, but a start. And if Axle was a member of the Lions, then getting to know everything about the man could lead to others in the group.

"Do you think Mrs. Hudson knows what her husband was up to? What got him killed?"

His image of Melora, frightened and vulnerable, didn't fit with her being a cold, calculating woman who approved of her husband's illegal activities. "I aim to find out. I don't think the intruder was there to rob her place. Oliver is tracking down the getaway car."

"Stay on her. Get to be her new best friend. Find out what she knows."

"That's what I plan on doing." As Daniel headed toward the door, his cell rang. Noticing the call came from the sheriff, he answered it as he left Ben's office. "Riley here."

"We're at Alicia Wells's apartment. I think you should come take a look at the place."

"She's not there?"

"Nope, and it appears she left in a hurry."

After the sheriff gave him the location of the apartment, Daniel slipped his cell into his pocket and started for the exit.

Oliver stopped him. "I tracked down the white Honda, at least I think it's the one. It was reported missing this morning. It belongs to Paul Carson."

"Has the car been found?"

"No."

"Check Carson out and interview him. The man I chased was compact, five feet nine inches with medium-length black hair. See if he fits the description."

Daniel hurried toward his truck. He felt as though Melora was the key to what was going on. He would stick to her like glue.

Thirty minutes later, he pulled into the parking lot of the building where Alicia Wells lived. When he entered the apartment, the sheriff waved him over and pointed at a spot on the rug, the size of a quarter. "Found this after I called you. We tested it. That's fresh blood."

THREE

"So you think it's human?" Daniel scanned Alicia Wells's living room.

"Yes. No signs of a pet. But the lab will have to confirm it and the blood type."

"Why do you think she ran?" Daniel spotted a desk with some open drawers.

The sheriff stiffened.

"Because her clothes and most of her personal belongings are gone. I didn't see this blood until a second walk-through."

"So you're thinking someone took her and made it look like she left?"

Sheriff Layton stroked his chin. "Possibly. I suppose there could be a simple explanation for the blood, like she cut herself. It certainly isn't enough to kill her." He flipped back the edge of the rug.

Daniel noticed several more spots of what looked like dried blood along that edge—not nearly enough to indicate she was seriously injured. But his gut feeling on this was they'd find Alicia dead.

He hoped he was wrong, but the people they were dealing with wouldn't hesitate to kill someone after they got what they wanted. "I'll have my office look into Alicia Wells if that's okay with you."

"Fine by me." The sheriff started for the bedroom. "I suspect Ms. Wells didn't go willingly."

"If Alicia gave someone the code and key to the house, that would explain the how of the break-in but not the why or the who."

"You don't think it was just a robbery attempt?"

"I think there's more to it. Possibly connected to Captain Pike's murder." Halting at the entrance into the room, Daniel surveyed the open drawers, the empty closet, the rumpled coverlet on the bed.

"All connected to Axle's body being found?"

"That's what I'm thinking. It was found at a drop site used by the group we think is responsible for Greg's death." Axle was somehow connected to the Lions of Texas, either he was one of them or he crossed one of them.

Daniel covered the distance to the closet and examined it—hangers tossed on the carpeted floor, a few clothing items still hanging on the rod, a box of papers scattered about the remaining three pairs of shoes. Kneeling by the mess, he took a pen out of his pocket and used it to move some of the pieces around.

"Look at this." Daniel glanced over his shoulder at the sheriff. "These are financial papers. If she was running, why didn't she take them with her?"

"Maybe she was interrupted and didn't have time to come back for them? Maybe that blood has been there for a while. Someone obviously tried to cover it up but missed the few spots on the rug. It kind of blends with the other colors."

"We'll need to look into her accounts and see if she's received any large amounts of money." Something out of the corner of his eye caught his attention. Leaning forward, Daniel poked under the shelving in the closet with his pen. He slid out a hundred dollar bill. "Or not. Cash works just as well."

Melora left the hospital gift shop after volunteering behind the counter. She had to keep up appearances, act as though nothing was wrong. And every Wednesday morning she helped in the auxiliary's gift shop. She didn't want to make anyone nervous.

Looking down, she opened her purse and dug around for her car keys. She nearly collided with Dr. Jorge Cantana, the father of Kaitlyn's friend Cara, but stopped herself one step short when she glanced back up.

Startled, he pulled his gaze away from a folder he

was reading, his dark hair tousled. "Sorry, Melora." His warm appraisal skimmed down her. "Where are you heading to? Finished volunteering?"

"Yes. I have a meeting at one for the Alamo Planning Committee. We're really getting geared up for a big celebration for the Battle of the Alamo anniversary."

"How do you keep everything straight?"

She withdrew her PDA from her purse. "By counting on this. What's got you flustered?"

"Flustered?"

She flipped her hand toward his white doctor coat, buttoned wrong.

He chuckled. "Oh." After fixing it, he peered up at Melora. "One of my patients isn't responding to his treatment. I'm trying to figure out what else I can do."

Jorge had been their family doctor for years. He was her uncle's doctor, too. He and his wife had been there for her after Axle had disappeared. He'd even tried to help her with Kaitlyn when his busy schedule allowed.

"Just remember to take some time for yourself. I worry about you working so hard."

He grinned. "Don't. I thrive on working. Thankfully, my wife understands."

"Tell Beth hi for me. I hope our daughters can get together again. Kaitlyn enjoys playing with Cara."

"That sounds like a good idea." He started to move away, stopped and turned back. "If you need to talk, I'm available. So is Beth. I know Axle has been gone for two years, and you felt something had happened to him, but now knowing for sure still has to be processed."

"I appreciate that." If she wasn't so afraid, she might actually have time to do that very thing. But all her energy had to be focused on keeping her daughter safe. Figuring out a way to get their lives back.

Checking her watch, Melora noticed she was running late for the meeting. She hurried from the hospital and located her silver Lexus in the parking lot. As she slid behind the steering wheel, she scouted the area. She couldn't find anyone watching her, but she felt it deep in her bones. She'd felt that way ever since Axle's body had been identified.

Who was watching her? Why were they watching? She wasn't going to talk. She didn't even have much she could tell the authorities. She didn't know the details of her husband's activities, and she planned to make that clear to the Texas Rangers.

Two years ago, the two men who had broken into her house had told her they were after a flash drive. They hadn't found it then and had thankfully left her unharmed but with a warning. Had the man broken into her house two days ago because of the police's renewed interest in Axle? Had they stopped looking for the flash drive because they'd thought Axle had it on him? Then when his body was discovered, they realized the device wasn't with him?

Her head throbbed with all the unanswered questions. She pulled out of the parking lot and drove toward the meeting's location.

She really didn't know whom to trust. *Trust in the Lord.* The thought popped into her head as she turned into the space at the side of the office building. She'd pleaded with the Lord to help her when everything had started falling apart three years ago. He obviously hadn't thought she was worth His trouble. So somehow she had to find a way out of this mess by herself.

On the elevator ride she composed herself. She couldn't let people know what was going on. She had to be in control, poised—play the role she'd been cast in.

When she stepped into the hallway on the tenth floor, she came face-to-face with Rangers Daniel Boone Riley and Anderson Michaels. She tried to hide her surprise mixed with concern, but Daniel's assessing gaze honed in on her. She remembered at the funeral last week the kindness in his eyes when they had connected with hers.

"It's nice to see you again." Daniel shifted toward

her. "I believe you've met Anderson Michaels. He came with me in October to this meeting."

"Yes, I remember him." At this moment, Daniel's look didn't convey the kindness she'd glimpsed at the gravesite but something else—determination. To dig into Axle's past and put her and Kaitlyn in danger.

Anderson nodded toward her. "Good to see you again, Mrs. Hudson."

Why are they here? Struggling to remain outwardly calm while she quietly panicked inside, she forced a smile. She clutched her purse straps tighter to still the trembling in her hand. "Is there a problem with the celebration?"

While Anderson went into the conference room at the end of the hallway, Daniel hung back with her. "Possibly. I'll explain everything inside. I was going to call you, but then I had to come to this meeting. Afterward, I'd like to talk with you. Let you know what I've come up with concerning your break-in."

She glanced up and down the corridor. Another committee member stepped off the elevator. Rodney Tanner caught sight of them and headed toward them.

"I thought I was late. I guess the meeting hasn't started yet. Good to see you, Melora." Rodney patted Daniel on the back. "And you, too, Daniel.

How's your mother doing? I haven't seen her lately."

"She's fine, sir. She went to the Caribbean a couple of weeks ago and just returned."

"I'll have to call her and make sure she doesn't need anything. I told your father I would keep an eye on her."

"We need to start the meeting." Hank Zarvy, the chairman of the committee, stuck his head out into the hallway.

Melora used that excuse to hurry ahead of Daniel and Rodney into the room. Taking the last vacant chair on the left, she was relieved when Daniel sat on the opposite side of the table. His eyes zoomed in on her as he removed his white cowboy hat and put it under his seat. She fought the urge to squirm and wrenched her gaze away from his.

After going through a list of items on the agenda, Hank closed the folder in front of him and looked toward Daniel. "I understand the Texas Rangers have some concerns and wanted to express them today at this meeting. You've got the floor, Daniel."

Hank, too, had been good friends with his father. Actually, Daniel knew half of the members personally. He hoped that would help him talk them into the changes the Texas Rangers proposed.

Daniel rose, chancing a look toward Melora.

She'd been avoiding eye contact the whole meeting. At the moment, she stared down at the paper before her. *What are you hiding?*

He cleared his throat and turned his attention to Hank. "We've looked over the plans for the celebration and feel we have to recommend that it be toned down in scope. We think a more intimate celebration will give anyone bent on causing trouble less opportunity to disrupt the event. It'll be easier to keep an eye on the crowd with a smaller function. We're concerned that with the vice president and the governor attending there could be problems with security, especially in light of the letter in October alluding to bad things happening if the celebration wasn't canceled and then the anonymous phone call Hank received a few weeks ago threatening problems. It doesn't appear the person has given up, and we haven't been able to locate him."

Everyone began talking at once. Hank held up his hand. "This has been in the planning stages for years. We can't all of a sudden change plans. What kind of message would we be sending to others? That we can be intimidated? No!" Hank brought his hand down flat on the oak table. "This is Texas and this celebration is important to the state, especially to San Antonio."

"But we celebrate the Alamo's anniversary every year. We can make this one smaller and have a bigger one next year." Daniel looked pointedly at each member of the committee, lingering on Melora for a few extra seconds.

"Celebrating the 176th anniversary doesn't have the same kind of ring as the 175th anniversary." Rodney frowned. "And what if we have a threatening letter next year? Do we just cancel the celebration altogether? No, just like the United States doesn't give in to terrorists, we won't give in to this blackmail. Beef up security. Find the person responsible for the threats."

A few others interjected their thoughts. One was in favor of scaling the celebration down while two others weren't.

Frustrated, Daniel surveyed each member's face and saw resolve not to buckle under any pressure—except for Melora and the woman next to her. Melora's gaze connected with Daniel's for a brief moment, and he saw understanding in those green depths. The visual link stirred feelings of protectiveness in him.

"I think you know how this committee feels, but we'll put it to a vote. All in favor of keeping the celebration as it's planned now, raise your hand." Hank surveyed the people at the table. "Eight to two. It looks like we'll leave it as is."

Daniel gave Melora a smile for her no vote and sat.

"We expect you and the other Rangers to make

the celebration as safe as possible." Hank directed a hard look at Daniel, then Anderson. "And we don't need knowledge of the letter and phone call getting out. They were both vague, nothing concrete. I don't want the press to get hold of them and build up the threat to more than it is. You know how they can be. Understand, Rangers Riley and Michaels?"

"Yes, sir," both he and Anderson said.

"Good. Since we're getting closer to the anniversary, we'll convene in two weeks at the same time. That concludes our meeting." Closing his notepad in front of him, Hank rose.

Daniel surged to his feet and headed for the door. Out in the hall he paused and turned to Anderson. "Go ahead without me. I'm going to try and talk with Melora Hudson."

"Gonna use your charm to get the lady to tell all?"

"I'm working on it." Daniel chuckled. According to his ex-wife, he had none.

Melora emerged from the meeting room and spotted Daniel. Her mouth tightened and her shoulders tensed. Quickly, she fastened her attention on the opening elevator door and started toward it.

Daniel moved into her path. "I want to thank you for your support in the meeting."

"You're welcome." She took a step away, feeling

trapped by the Ranger's presence yet wanting to know if he'd discovered anything about Axle's death. Anything that could put her in more danger.

"I think the decision is a big mistake."

"I agree. It isn't necessary to take needless risks." She had enough of them to fill a lifetime.

"With added security there won't be needless risks," Rodney said, stopping next to Melora. He directed his look to Daniel. "I'm confident that the Texas Rangers will have the security needed to protect the public, the governor and the vice president. Look at the Super Bowl. The World Series. They manage to have those huge events without incident."

Daniel donned his cowboy hat. "We'll do the best job possible. But we wouldn't be doing that job if we didn't propose a smaller celebration for safety reasons."

"Son, I was good friends with your father. As you know, he loved this celebration. We'll miss him this year. He was looking forward to the event, had even pushed it before his death last year. He was passionate about anything to do with the Alamo. A true Texan to the core. We're dedicating this to your father and his memory."

The color leaked from Daniel's tanned features. "I'd heard that."

Daniel's father had been a big supporter of the

Alamo, the committee and San Antonio. He'd given large sums of money to various events to promote the city and state.

Rodney slapped Daniel on the back. "It's going to be okay, son. Nothing has ever happened before." The older man nodded toward Melora. "If there's anything I can do for you, please let me know. I'm sorry to hear about Axle, but at least now you have some closure."

A lump formed in her throat. Closure? She didn't know if she ever would. As Rodney ambled toward the elevator, Melora glanced around and noticed the hallway was empty except for them. In Daniel's dark gray eyes she glimpsed a vulnerability that she could identify with. The mention of his father had changed his bearing. For a few seconds his expression reflected pain as Rodney had talked. But also something else? Hurt was something she knew about. That connected them in a way she couldn't afford. She needed to distance herself as far from the police as possible. She didn't want the people watching her to think she was cooperating with the authorities.

Daniel blew a breath out. "Mom is happy about the dedication."

"But not you?"

"I don't know what I think." That hurt she'd sensed a few minutes ago inched back into his voice. "Especially if something does go wrong at the celebration."

"Rodney did spring it on you."

"Yeah. I'm not big on surprises."

"Neither am I," Melora said.

"Would you like some coffee? There's a café downstairs that makes a good cup."

"I probably need to—"

"Please."

The appeal in his expression touched her heart. No one was around. If someone was watching the building, they wouldn't know she'd had coffee with Daniel. And she wanted to know if he knew anything about Axle's case. Talking with him in a public place would be better than him coming to the house. From what she knew about Ranger Daniel Riley, their conversation a couple of days ago wouldn't be their last. She got the feeling he would keep visiting her until he got what he was after and that worried her a lot. The intruder's warning about the police resounded in her mind.

"Sure. I have a little time before I need to be home."

Daniel smiled, the corners of his eyes crinkling. "That's great."

His expression caused her heartbeat to increase. What would it feel like to have a normal life?

As she stepped up to the elevator, Daniel reached around her and punched the down button. Her stomach clenched at his nearness. A whiff of his fresh aftershave swirled around her. What she knew of him made her wish they'd met under different circumstances. For just a moment, she felt safe in his presence—a feeling she hadn't experienced in years.

They'd once moved in the same social circles, although Daniel hadn't attended many functions in the past five or six years. Rumor had it that he and his father, who died last year, had a falling out about his job in law enforcement. Was that what was behind the hurt and pain in his expression earlier?

The ding of the elevator pulled her away from her thoughts. She needed to keep her wits about her. She couldn't let him know what was going on and risk something happening to her daughter or uncle.

Inside the Java Hut, Melora ordered a chai latte while Daniel got a cup of black coffee. She sat at a table for four and decided it wasn't big enough. He was too close. Too commanding. Too appealing. Those thoughts stunned her. It had to be her exhaustion talking, what with the identification of Axle's body, his funeral, the break-in and new threats.

"Will the Rangers be able to secure the celebration?" she asked after taking a sip of her drink.

"We'll have to. We have no choice now. While

the secret service will guard the vice president, our main concern will be the governor and lieutenant governor." He set his mug on the placemat before him. "I'm glad you're here. I was going to pay you a visit to let you know about the progress on the break-in."

The mention of the intruder stiffened her spine. She gripped her cup, relishing the warmth on her cold fingers. "You found him?"

"No, but we think Alicia Wells was the one responsible for giving him a key and the code."

"Not Alicia. She's worked for me since I married Axle six years ago. She's never given me a reason to doubt her loyalty."

"Well, she's gone. Her bank account was closed two days ago. She deposited several thousand dollars late last week into it. Do you know any reason she would be putting that kind of money into her account? From the looks of her apartment, I didn't get the impression she had a lot of money."

"She works hard, but she's had some problems with her two kids."

"Do you know where they live?"

"She told me her son, Nate, was going to move to Dallas. He should have by now. Her daughter lives in San Diego. She was getting married, and Alicia didn't like the man. She said he was trouble."

"What's his name? The daughter's?" Daniel pulled out his notepad.

Seeing him write something on the paper, Melora glimpsed the patrons in the café. Two others were in the restaurant and had been there since they had come in. The couple's attention remained on each other. "Pedro something. I don't know his last name. Her daughter is Bella. You think Alicia went to one of her children?"

"Possibly. I need to check everything out."

"It was just a break-in—nothing taken," Melora said without thinking, reliving the terror she'd experienced with the intruder on Monday. Her heartbeat thundered in her ears. Her breathing became shallow.

"But what if the break-in is tied to your husband's murder?"

"Why? That's what you keep asking. He was killed two years ago." She had to remain calm and in control or Daniel would know she was hiding something for sure.

"Call it a hunch if you want."

The ever-present fear boiled in Melora's stomach. How could she get him to drop the investigation? "This past month has been very difficult, and I don't want any more grief. I just want to live in peace." That last sentence felt wrenched from her as though if she said it enough, it might happen. Peace. She longed for it.

"What if it's connected to Axle's murder and

the intruder was looking for something now that your husband has turned up dead?"

"Why would you say that?" As much as she tried, panic laced each word. She knew what the intruder was searching for—the flash drive.

"Because it looks like the intruder went to some lengths to break into your place. If it was an ordinary robber, why would he possibly pay your maid for your key and code? Wouldn't he just find an easier target?"

Melora was in over her head and she didn't know what to do. These people meant business. How could she say anything to Daniel and keep her family safe? She didn't know where the flash drive was or anything about Axle's business. "You don't know that for sure. Maybe Alicia just decided to live with one of her children, or maybe she's somewhere else. She isn't due at my house until tomorrow. Maybe she'll show up." Although she knew that wasn't the case. Alicia wouldn't have left without telling her.

Daniel scribbled a note on his paper. When his eyes connected with hers, a storm brewed in their depths. "What are you really afraid of, Melora?"

FOUR

"Shouldn't I be afraid? Someone murdered my husband. That's not something that happens to most people. I have a daughter to think about. Who knows what they were after or wanted? What will finding my husband's body do to the person who killed him?" That was as close to the truth she would tell Daniel Riley, and she realized by the glimmer that sparked his eyes it had been too much. But she was so tired of doing this alone, and frankly, she didn't know what to do anymore.

He leaned close, his gaze diamond hard. "So you do know something?"

"I didn't say that." She cradled her mug between her palms and hoped she didn't slosh her chai latte as she brought it to her lips. She sipped, but the tea's warmth did nothing to heat her cold insides.

"If you're in danger, I can help."

Your presence puts me in danger. What if they think I'm helping you? "I'm fine. I just want to get back to a normal life with Kaitlyn." That had to be her total focus. She took another swallow of her latte, then set the mug on the table, keeping her hands around it. "You don't have any clue who broke into my house?"

"Not yet. Alicia is missing. No one has seen her in two days and some blood was found at her place. It has been confirmed by the lab that it was human."

Alicia's blood? Was she dead, too? The thud of Melora's heart echoed through her, drowning out the sounds around her. She saw Daniel's mouth moving, but she didn't hear his words. His concern finally pierced through her veil of disbelief and fear. "She's dead?" she asked in a whisper.

"Don't know. No bodies at the morgue fit her description. I've checked the hospitals, and she hasn't been admitted."

"But you said her blood was found at her apartment?"

"It was her blood type but not enough to indicate a mortal wound. If it was hers, she didn't bleed out at her place."

"But she might have somewhere else?" The very thought scared her even more. If she said anything, that could be her blood, her daughter's, Juanita's or her uncle's.

"We don't know, but it doesn't look good. That several thousand dollars she received right before the break-in is definitely a red flag to me. Would her children give her that kind of money?"

Melora shook her head. "They wouldn't have it. They're struggling. She was trying to help them. Not the other way around." Is that why Alicia might have given someone her key and code? *Oh, Alicia, I would have helped you if you had asked me.* "Do you know anything else?"

"The car the intruder used was stolen. The owner reported it stolen. It doesn't look like he's involved in any way."

"Have you found the car?"

"No, but it'll probably turn up abandoned somewhere."

"Is there a chance you can get any evidence from it?"

He shrugged. "It's possible, but the man was wearing gloves, so unless he took them off to drive, it's doubtful we'll find prints. But why should you care? You said you didn't want to press charges even if we found him."

"I said I want this to be over with. Besides, nothing was taken, and I didn't see the man's face. I don't see how you could get a conviction."

"You make that sound like good news."

The drill of his gaze bore through her. For a few seconds she wanted to tell him everything. But the intruder's threat replayed through her mind and the words stuck in her throat. "I think I'm just trying to be a realist and not get my hopes up," she finally said.

She needed to get out of here. How did she think she could have a conversation with the Texas Ranger and leave unscathed? He already thought she was lying to him. She wished she knew where the flash drive was hidden. If she found it, she might have a bargaining chip—something she could give to the police and hopefully end this nightmare.

"The Rangers at Company D are dedicated to getting to the truth. Our captain was murdered, too. We take care of our own." His stare, if it were possible, hardened even more.

Melora swallowed with difficulty, leaving a dryness in her throat. "And I take care of my own." She shot to her feet. "I need to go. My daughter went to kindergarten today and will be home soon." Looping her purse strap over her shoulder, she clutched the handbag to her. "Thanks for the latte."

When she started for the exit, Daniel quickly followed her. The urge to put some distance between them almost overruled her common sense. Running away from him would only send up more red flags.

"Where's your car?" He fell into step next to her.

She scanned the street. Was that man across the

street watching her? When the person in question turned, put some money into a newspaper stand, withdrew the latest edition then entered the building three feet away, she released a long breath. But then she spied another young man lounging against a brick wall, his gaze on her. She hurried her pace. The faster she could get out of here the better off she would be.

A few yards from her silver Lexus, one of her three-inch high heels got caught in a hole in the concrete. She stumbled, flailing her arms to stop herself from falling. Daniel grabbed her and wrapped his arms around her middle to steady her, her back pressed against his chest.

"Okay," he said against the side of her neck.

His hot breath scorched her flesh, making her vividly aware of the man behind her. She wanted to melt into the safety of his arms. Then she remembered the other man across the street and wrenched herself from his loose embrace, whirling about to face him. "I'm fine. I don't need your help."

One eyebrow arched. "You don't? I should have let you fall then?"

Yes. You should have stayed inside, she wanted to shout at him. *What if they're watching? What if they think there's something between us?* Those questions tumbled through her mind. She funneled her trembling fingers through her hair.

His nostrils flared at the sight of her shaking

hands. He seized them and moved closer. "I can protect you, Melora. What are you afraid of? What do you know?"

She wanted to believe he could protect her and Kaitlyn—the rest of the people she cared about, but Axle had been so capable of taking care of himself, even had a bodyguard who protected him. And someone had gotten to him. Murdered him. "I'm fine. Good day, Ranger Riley."

She pivoted toward her car, fumbled in her purse for her keys and then slipped behind the steering wheel. When she switched on her engine, Daniel knocked on her window and motioned for her to roll it down. She wanted to press her foot on the accelerator and speed out of the parking lot, but his hand was on the door handle.

She pressed the button. The window slid down, and she got a whiff of his clean lime scent. "I don't want to be late."

"Just in case you lost my card, here's another one with my home and cell numbers on the back. Call me any time of the day if you need me or want to talk." He offered the card to her.

She snatched it and started to roll the window back up but paused. "I do have a question for you. What happened to Axle's bodyguard, Gordon Johnson? When Axle disappeared, he did, too. I never heard from him or saw him again. I mentioned that to the sheriff. They looked for him, but I never heard about him."

"You think Gordon Johnson killed your husband?"

"It's a possibility. Or..." She shuddered at the other likelihood—that another man was dead besides Axle.

He cocked one corner of his mouth upward, but his eyes remained cold. "Are you throwing me a bone so I won't bother you anymore?"

"I kind of think of you as a pit bull. I don't see you getting swayed by a mere bone. But you deal with that bit of information any way you want. I hadn't thought about Gordon in a while. I figured he left town when the man he was supposed to guard disappeared."

He straightened and tipped his cowboy hat. "Good day, Melora. I'll be speaking to you soon."

She rolled the window up and pulled out of the parking space with Daniel watching her drive away. The young man across the street still leaned against the building, scanning the street, his arms and legs crossed while he smoked a cigarette. As she turned into the flow of traffic, the young man grinned. A grin that reached into her chest and squeezed her heart in terror.

Later that evening Melora stood in the entrance to Axle's office, surveying the territory that he'd made clear she wasn't to disturb. Was the information in here somewhere? She looked right after the first break-in but found nothing. Although those first intruders had told her that Axle was dead, she hadn't done anything to the office in case the men had been wrong. For months after that, she'd imagined Axle showing up one day, wanting to reclaim everything.

Now she needed to do something with the office. Box up the items. Get them out of her house. Erase Axle's presence from her life.

"Mommy, where are you?"

Melora backed into the hallway. "I'm here in your daddy's office."

Kaitlyn's footsteps pattered on the tile as she ran from the kitchen and across the wide foyer. She skidded to a stop, frowning. "I can't find Patches. I've looked everywhere."

"All his hiding places?"

Her daughter nodded.

"Maybe he's still outside." They had a small pet door he used when he wanted to go out, but usually he stayed in the house. "Sometimes he likes to go exploring in the neighborhood."

"It's dinnertime. He never misses that."

Melora checked her watch, surprised that it was already six o'clock. "It's later than I thought." She spent the afternoon thinking about Daniel and the man across the street watching her. She couldn't shake the grin of malice she'd glimpsed from the young man nor the warm feel of Daniel's hands on her.

"Mommy, we have to find Patches. He'll be hungry."

Melora settled her hand on Kaitlyn's shoulder. "Honey, he'll come home when he's hungry enough. Leave the food. We'll see him shortly, I'm sure." In all the time they'd had the cat, he'd always found his way home. He was probably in the backyard stalking a bird or squirrel. Thankfully, she'd never seen him catch one.

"Let's go see when dinner is going to be tonight. Remember Uncle Tyler is coming over to eat with us?"

"Oh, good. I can show him my new book. Maybe he'll read it to me." Kaitlyn took Melora's hand and tugged her toward the kitchen.

Stepping into the room, Melora drew in a deep breath. The prime rib smelled wonderful. Coupled with the aroma of Juanita's delicious homemade biscuits, Melora's taste buds were actually tempted, something that hadn't happened in weeks—ever since the body had been found.

"When will Señor Madison be here?" Juanita turned the stove on to steam her vegetables.

"Any minute. Can you hold dinner for a while? I want to talk to him before we eat."

The doorbell chimed. Kaitlyn whirled about and yelled as she raced toward the foyer, "I'll get it."

"Wait, honey, let—" But her daughter was at the door, thrusting it open before Melora could finish her sentence.

"You're *finally* here." Kaitlyn launched herself into her great uncle's arms.

Melora slowed her pace when she heard her uncle greet Kaitlyn, but she would have to talk with her daughter about opening the door like that. What if that hadn't been Uncle Tyler but that man watching her earlier? He could have snatched…

"Good evening, Melora."

She blinked, suddenly realizing her uncle was standing in front of her, holding her daughter in his arms. The sight of him brought relief to her. She was safe with him here this evening. But she knew that feeling would only be fleeting. After all he'd done for her, taking her in and raising her, she wouldn't endanger his life.

"Kaitlyn, Juanita could use some help with the dessert. Can you give her a hand? There'll be time later to talk to Uncle Tyler."

Her uncle placed her daughter on the floor. "Don't forget I get to read that new book to you tonight before you go to bed."

Kaitlyn raced for the kitchen, saying, "I won't."

The second she was gone her uncle's sharp gaze

zeroed in on Melora. "What's wrong? Still not sleeping?"

She shook her head. "So much has been happening with Axle's funeral, the reading of the will, the…" A knot formed in her throat. Tears jammed behind it.

Cradling her hands between his, Uncle Tyler moved close. "I'm here for you. What do you need?"

Moisture misted her eyes. "I need to get rid of Axle's things. I want to sell the restaurant chain, too. Can you help me?"

"Of course, but are you sure you want to get rid of the business? It's making good money."

She didn't want to tell her uncle the reason why she needed to sell the restaurants. She didn't want to drag him into anything that could be dangerous. "I need to invest the money, with your help, in something I can understand. I don't know the first thing about running a chain like Axle's."

"You don't have to. That's why I hired William Thompson to run the business for you."

She drew herself up straighter, to stress she wasn't going to let Uncle Tyler talk her into anything she knew she shouldn't do. "I want to be able to comprehend what's going on. Weren't you the one who said know what you're getting into before you take the plunge?"

He laughed. "Yeah, but that was the time you

dove into the lake from the bluff. You could have hurt yourself if it hadn't been deep enough or there had been rocks under the water."

"The same principle applies." She hooked her arm through his and headed for Axle's office.

At the door, Uncle Tyler stopped and angled toward her. "Look, I can buy the restaurant chain from you. It would be a good investment for me."

"No, it wouldn't," Melora said without thought.

He frowned. "You forget I've looked at the books and know what's going on. I didn't turn it over to William without watching out for your interests."

But if something illegal was going on, she didn't want her uncle tied up in it. She forced a smile to her lips. "You know nothing has to be settled right away. We have plenty of time to figure out what to do with the business. Maybe after the holidays."

As he smiled the sparkle in his dark eyes showcased the appeal her uncle could exert effortlessly. His dignified look combined with his tall stature commanded people's attention when he entered a room. Much like Daniel did. Like at today's committee meeting. Even though Hank hadn't gone along with what Daniel had requested concerning the Alamo celebration, she'd seen the respect in the older man's expression when dealing with Daniel.

"Why are we in here," Uncle Tyler waved his arm toward the office, "when I can smell Juanita's delicious roast?"

"Before you came, I was in here thinking about what to do with Axle's personal belongings now that he's officially dead."

Bushy white eyebrows slashed downward. "What?"

Melora laid her hand on his arm. "I know how much you liked Axle, but I've got to move on."

"Are you getting rid of all this?"

"Probably not right away but after the holidays. I don't want to disrupt Kaitlyn's Christmas. This past week has been tough enough on her."

"And not you?"

She didn't want to lie to her uncle, but neither could she tell him the whole truth. "When Axle didn't come home, I felt something was wrong. After a year, I came to accept that he was gone— probably dead. His body being found actually brought some closure for me." Suddenly, she had a thought that slammed into her like the intruder who had tackled her to the floor. What if she found Axle's flash drive? What would she do with it? Whatever she did could have far-reaching conse- quences, and above all she could never put her family in danger. She would have to consider it carefully.

Melora backed out of the office and closed its

door as though if she didn't see Axle's possessions she wouldn't be faced with the dilemma. "You're right. We can wait to talk about the business and Axle's things. Dinner should be ready. I know how much you like Juanita's cooking."

"Sometimes I can't believe you persuaded me to let you hire Juanita away from me."

She was thankful every day that he'd graciously giving his blessing for Juanita to come to work for her. The housekeeper had been the only person who knew what had really gone on in the house with Axle. That she and Axle weren't the perfect couple they had presented to the world. That her marriage had been held together with threats.

As they entered the kitchen area, Kaitlyn stood by the pet door. Her mouth dipped in a frown. "Patches still hasn't returned. Should I put his food in his bowl?"

"Go ahead, honey. He may come back while we're eating dinner and want his own."

"Okay." With one last look at the pet door, Kaitlyn trudged toward the utility room, her shoulders slumped.

"What's wrong?" Uncle Tyler asked as he watched his niece disappear.

"Patches hasn't come home. She's worried."

"Does he often stay out this late?"

"Not usually. But you know cats are independent, especially male ones."

Kaitlyn reentered the kitchen as Juanita placed the sliced roast on a serving platter. "Dinner is served. Kaitlyn, you need to wash up."

Melora held out her hand to her daughter, saying, "Let's go do it together," and made her way toward the mudroom.

Inside it she looked at the entrance that Daniel used to bust into the house two days ago. There were no signs of forced entry now because the door had been replaced with a steel-reinforced one—not one easily kicked in. As she turned on the water for her daughter, she wished she could forget that day, but she couldn't. The young man she'd seen watching her today only supported that.

The next morning after Juanita left to take Kaitlyn to school, Melora sat at the kitchen table drinking a cup of tea and trying to decide what she should do. Uncle Tyler again told her right before he'd left last night that he didn't want to see her sell the restaurant chain, but if she was determined to, that he would buy it. She didn't want her uncle caught up in Axle's illegal activities. She had to protect him.

Lord, I know I haven't talked to You in a while, but I need Your help. What do I do? I know this is cliché, but I feel like I'm drowning and going down for the third time. Please help me.

Melora closed her eyes and savored the quiet,

wishing it brought her the peace she so wanted. Something hit the tiled floor and her eyes bolted open. She scanned the kitchen and saw nothing until her gaze fell on to Patches's black collar at the bottom of the pet door.

"Patches?"

Silence returned.

She surged to her feet, nearly knocking over her chair in her haste. Covering the few feet to the bay window that overlooked the back yard, she peered outside. A flash at the side of her house secured her attention. Patches? Something else? Or someone else?

The idea that a person had come up to her back door and pushed something through the small pet door knotted her stomach into a hard ball. She moved to the collar and picked it up, examining it for any hints of how it came to be on her floor. That was when she saw a red X across Patches's tag. The collar tumbled from her grasp and struck the tiles again with a clunk.

FIVE

An hour later Melora prowled the kitchen, not able to sit, not able to think clearly. Was Patches dead? The red hadn't been blood but a Magic Marker. She'd hidden the collar in a drawer. She didn't want Kaitlyn to see it. She felt helpless.

Continuing to pace, she passed the wall phone and glanced at it. Call Daniel. Tell him what was going on. Maybe he could protect her, help her.

No, his presence would only make it worse. Hadn't she been warned enough? Wasn't Patches's disappearance a clear threat?

She again circled the room, too restless to sit, her nerve endings on fire. She needed to figure out how she was going to tell Kaitlyn that Patches might…

A cry pierced the air, twisting Melora toward the back door. Patches shot through the pet opening and raced across the room. He hurled himself into her arms, his whines beautiful music to her ears. Burying her face in his fur, she breathed in the scent of the outdoors and smoke.

The memory of the man watching her at the Riverwalk, a cigarette in his hand, made her tremble. Had he taken Patches? As much as he exasperated her at times, having Patches in her arms was wonderful. Could the Lord be sending her a message of hope? She so needed it.

Finally having enough petting, the cat squirmed until she placed him on the floor, and he moseyed into the utility room where she heard him munching on his food. She wished she could right her world that easily.

With a sigh, she grabbed her cold cup of tea sitting on the table and pitched its contents into the sink. She still didn't know what to do. Maybe if she called Daniel and only talked to him over the phone, stressing how important it was that they didn't meet in person....

The doorbell chiming intruded into her thoughts. She wasn't expecting anyone. Quickly, she planted herself at the window in the dining room that afforded her a view of the porch and driveway that circled in front of her house. The white Ford 150 truck mocked her. Then she saw Daniel standing in broad daylight for the world to see on her porch.

Why did he have to come to her house?

The chimes rang again, and she hurried to answer the door. Maybe she could get rid of him, and no one would be the wiser that he was here. But then she remembered the person who had dropped Patches's collar through her pet door only an hour ago and knew someone was probably watching her place right now, especially since her cat had just been returned.

Why couldn't the man have better timing? Or better yet, no timing.

Melora wrenched open the front door, coming face-to-face with a Ranger who filled her entrance with his presence, full of power and self-confidence. Her eyes fixed on the gun holstered at his waist, and she resolved not to do or say something she would regret.

"To what do I owe this…visit?"

"I had some news on the break-in."

"The one where nothing was taken."

His mouth tightened. "Only because I interrupted the man. Can I come in?"

No, go away. With difficulty she held those words inside and said, "For a few minutes. I was on my way out."

He stepped over the threshold. "I won't be too long. I just have a few more questions."

Starting to shut the door, she gripped its edge tighter. "I thought you were giving me an update."

"That, too." He grinned, the shadow from the brim of his cowboy hat shading part of his face.

For some reason she didn't think his smile reached his eyes. Instead of going into the living room and sitting, Melora swept around after securing the door and planted herself in the foyer, crossing her arms over her chest. "What did you drive all the way out here to tell me?"

"The getaway car was found abandoned about five miles from here. What fingerprints found in it could be accounted for with the owner and his family."

"So there wasn't anything in it to help you find the person who broke in?"

"I didn't say that."

Patience. She got the feeling that Daniel was purposefully trying her. "Then what else?"

"A phone number on a scrap of paper that the owner didn't recognize, and he's the only one who drives the car. He'd cleaned it out a couple of weeks ago, and other than his wife, no one else had been in it since then. She didn't know anything about the phone number, either."

She pointedly checked her watch. "So you think it belonged to the guy in my house."

"A definite possibility." His smile grew, and this time she was sure it touched his dark depths. "I called it."

She fortified herself with a deep breath. "And?"

"It was one of your husband's restaurants. The

one on the Riverwalk downtown. Have you ever been to that restaurant? Do you know any of the employees there?"

"Oh, is this the question part of your visit?"

He cocked his head. "I do believe it is."

"Yes to the first question and no to the second one."

"You've been there, but don't know any of the employees of a restaurant you own?"

"*My husband* owned. The last time I went to that restaurant, the first one in his chain, was three years ago on its tenth anniversary. I know the manager changed shortly after that, and I never met the new one."

"You haven't been back to his premier restaurant since then?"

Dropping her arms to her sides, she drew herself up straight and looked him in the eye. "Yes. I told you I don't know anything about my husband's business. You'll need to talk to the man overseeing it now if you have a question about it. That's William Thompson."

His eyes narrowed and filled with doubt. "How convenient to deny any knowledge about your *dead* husband's affairs."

The ruthless way he said dead shivered down her length. At that moment she wondered who was more dangerous—Daniel Riley or the unknown person watching her. The truth—what little she knew—needed to be shared with him, but she couldn't say the words. They clogged her throat like talons around her vocal cords.

"I'm sorry, but I was one of those wives that ran the home and let her husband run his business." Because that was the way Axle wanted it—not her.

"You aren't worried about what happened the other day?"

Yes, I'm terrified. But if she revealed that, she would be grilled with more questions she didn't have answers to. "Of course I'm concerned about the attempted robbery and have taken measures to secure my house better." Again, she made a big deal out of glancing at her watch. "Now, if you'll excuse—"

The blare of the phone charged the air. She flinched, not expecting the sound, but used the interruption to hurry into the living room to answer the call.

"Hello."

"Hello, Melora."

She stiffened. The same voice—raspy, smoke-saturated—as the man who had broken into her house. She turned her back on Daniel and lowered her voice. "What do you want?"

"I see you have company. I see taking Patches wasn't enough. I'm through giving you warnings."

"I haven't said anything."

"Good, because Kaitlyn is a pretty little girl. We wouldn't want anything to happen to her—or you." Click.

Daniel listened to Melora's murmured voice, too quiet for him to hear what she was saying. He strode toward the door the intruder had used, pretending an interest in its new lock. He slid a glance back toward her, her face pale, her hands locked around the phone. Terror looked back at him.

"Thanks for reminding me. I should be there shortly. I was detained but he was just leaving. Bye." She replaced the receiver in its cradle, lowering her eyelids to veil her expression.

"I'll ask you again. What are you hiding?" *Tell me. Please.*

Her look stabbed him. "Nothing. Now I really have to go."

"Are you all right?" When her eyelids lifted, the terror was gone, but he sensed it was only banked until he left.

She shook her head as though ridding her mind of something distasteful. "I will be when you leave." For the third time she glanced at her watch.

If the situation wasn't so serious, he would laugh at the woman's poor attempts to convince him she knew nothing and was late for some appointment.

He sauntered toward her, took a business card from his pocket and stuffed it into her palm. "Just in case you lost the other ones."

She grabbed his hand, her eyes widening slightly, and returned the card. "I don't need it. Save a tree."

The warm feel of her fingers on his jolted him. He snatched his hand back with the slip of paper in it. "Suit yourself. If I have any more questions, I'll be in touch."

"Next time use the phone. It'll save you the gas coming all the way out here for nothing."

"Another green tip." He tapped the brim of his cowboy hat. "I appreciate the thought. Good day, Melora." He started forward, paused and glanced back. "I thought I'd let you know that we're looking around the area where your husband was found for his bodyguard. But investigating other possibilities, too. Thanks for the information about Gordon Johnson."

Her eyes brightened for a few seconds before she masked her surprise.

As he walked to the door, he noticed her purse sitting on a table nearby. He detoured and stuck the card she'd given back to him into the side of the bag. "Humor me," he said when she opened her mouth to say something.

Without uttering a word, she grasped the handle and opened the door. Its closing behind him the second he stepped over the threshold couldn't strictly be considered a slam but only a decibel or two off. He chuckled. He had her rattled and maybe she would finally slip and admit something wasn't right. *Ask me for help.* He threw a look over his shoulder at the heavy wooden door. *Please, before something bad happens to you.*

He started for his truck, panning the terrain before him. Melora was scared. Who had called and what had the person said to make her go white like that? His survey brought him no answers. Nothing out of the ordinary. At least nothing visible.

Melora bolted the front door and even went to the alarm system and turned it on. If someone came into her house, she would know it.

Then the full implications of what the man on the phone had said hit her. He thought she was talking to the Texas Rangers. He knew the name of her cat and her daughter. He inserted all the personal information to unnerve her more. And his plan had worked.

She collapsed onto the couch in the living room and squeezed her hands together so tightly her knuckles were white. Pain streaked up her arms from her locked muscles. Who was she kidding? Staying here wouldn't keep her safe. She had to get away with Kaitlyn. They would harass her and hound her until she turned over what they wanted. And since she couldn't give them what she didn't have, they would be forced to accelerate their terror tactics, which meant her daughter was in danger.

Finger combing her hair, she tried to think of a way to get away undetected. Start over somewhere else—as far from here as possible. She would have to get some money without being obvious and pack some of their belongings. Although clothes could be purchased wherever they ended up, there were a few things Kaitlyn would miss if she didn't get to take them with her.

Please, Lord, I'm begging You to help me.

"Mommy, why are you coming into my school?" Kaitlyn held Melora's hand as they marched toward the entrance Monday morning.

"We're going on an adventure."

"Is that why I have my favorite toys in my backpack?"

"You're so sharp, sweetheart." Melora walked past the office and headed for the doors on the other side of the school. "I've got a cab picking us up so we can start our adventure." But before charging out of the exit, she scanned the parking lot for anything unusual other than the waiting taxi.

If her plan worked, whoever was watching her

would be looking for her to come back outside in an hour since she often volunteered at her daughter's school. That would give Kaitlyn and her some time to get out of San Antonio. She clutched her large purse under one arm and clasped Kaitlyn's hand again before stepping outside.

Rushing toward the cab, Melora did a visual sweep of the area, but she didn't see anything unusual. At the taxi, she wrenched opened the door, guided her daughter in first then joined her in the backseat.

After giving the driver the address of a car rental place where she had a reserved vehicle, she laid her arm on Kaitlyn's shoulder and pressed her against her side. "Here we go. This is gonna be fun." She forced a lightness into her voice while the clenching of her muscles mocked her words.

But not ten minutes later while the cab was speeding down the highway, a large navy truck came alongside the taxi and began inching into their lane. The taxi driver lay on his horn, but the pickup kept coming until it bumped against the side, near Melora's door. She swallowed a scream, not wanting to frighten Kaitlyn any more than the loud, crunching sound of the truck connecting with the cab already had. The pickup's dark tinted windows prevented her from seeing the driver.

"Mommy!"

Melora cuddled her daughter closer to her. "Shh, baby, it's gonna be okay."

"Hey, get over, buddy," the taxi driver shouted and pressed down on the accelerator.

For a few seconds he shot out ahead of the truck. Until it collided with the back bumper, sending Melora and Kaitlyn forward only to have their seatbelts catch and throw them back against the seat.

Another slam into the rear right side and the cab driver lost control of his vehicle. It flew off the road and bounced over the rougher terrain alongside the highway. Kaitlyn's sobs iced her blood while sweat beaded Melora's brow.

"I'm here, honey." Heart pounding, Melora cradled Kaitlyn next to her and braced herself for the impact with the fence.

As Daniel grabbed a cup of coffee and started back toward his office, Rangers Gisella Hernandez and Evan Chen came into the reception area. He paused in his trek, taking a long sip of his coffee. "What did you two find out?"

"No one on staff at the restaurant fits the description you gave us of the driver of the white Honda." Tall with dark hair and eyes, Gisella stopped near Daniel while Evan made his way toward the coffeepot. When he lifted the glass carafe and looked toward Gisella, she said, "I'll take some."

"Anyone recently quit who did?" Daniel leaned against the edge of the receptionist's desk.

"Nope." Gisella took the mug Evan handed her.

"That's what I was afraid of. It was a long shot, but I was hoping he worked there. More likely he was calling an accomplice." Daniel crossed his legs as he sipped more of his brew. He wished that for once something on this case would come easy.

"Or the person who hired him," Evan said.

"I want you two to dig into the backgrounds of everyone working at the restaurant. See if there is any connection to the others we know are involved in this case. I'm going to have a conversation with the William Thompson who runs the chain for the widow." As the pair of Rangers headed for their offices, Daniel immediately pictured Melora's ashen features the last time he was at her house. The person on the other end of the phone line had said something that had scared her. His gut told him she was in trouble. Whether she liked it or not, he would stay close.

He stopped at Oliver's cubicle and waited for the Ranger to finish his call.

Oliver glanced toward him as he hung up. "I've been trying to locate Gordon Johnson. No one has heard from him in two years."

"Keep looking. He might have been involved in

his boss's murder. Let me know if the search at the animal rescue center unearths another body. I also want you to work on getting a warrant to wiretap Melora Hudson's phone." Daniel didn't think they had the evidence yet to do it, but he couldn't shake her frightened image from his mind.

Oliver nodded. Daniel swallowed a few more sips of his coffee and went to his office to put his mug on his desk before leaving. No time like the present to see what Mr. Thompson knew.

His cell rang as he stepped outside. Quickly he answered it. "Riley here."

"This is Mercy Hospital. Melora Hudson and her daughter were brought into the emergency room. She asked me to call you."

"Emergency room? What happened?" He lengthened his strides toward his truck in the parking lot.

"They were in a wreck."

Daniel went cold. His gut knotted. "I'll be right there."

Her body aching, Melora stood at the end of the bed in the emergency room as the doctor and nurse finished up with Kaitlyn. Melora fought the tears threatening her composure. She couldn't do this anymore. They could have been killed today. The cab driver might have been. All she knew was that they'd rushed him into surgery.

The sounds around her faded to be replaced with remembered ones from the crash—the crunch of metal, a hissing noise, her daughter's cries when something came through the windshield, shattering the glass. She hugged her arms to her chest but nothing warded off the cold that encased her.

"Melora, are you all right?" Daniel appeared at her side.

She hadn't even seen him enter the room in the E.R. She wanted to go into his arms—have them encircle her in a ring of protection. She stayed where she was, tightening the hold on herself. "Yes—no." The last word came out in a squeak as the doctor finished cleaning the cuts on her daughter's face, Kaitlyn's wide eyes glued to hers, tears swimming in them.

"I'm here to help." He slipped his arm across her shoulder and brought her against him.

She didn't resist. She grasped on to what he said, hoping she was making the right decision because what she had done so far hadn't kept her and her daughter safe.

"Do you want to tell me what happened?"

Melora peered at Kaitlyn. "Later. Right now I need to get my daughter home."

Jorge Cantana came into the room. "Melora, I just heard you and Kaitlyn were here. What happened?"

When she saw her best friend's father, Kaitlyn

burst out crying. Melora shook her head at Jorge and rounded the end of the bed to draw her daughter into her arms.

"Baby, I'm right here. You'll be good as new in no time." Melora kissed the top of Kaitlyn's hair, the scent of antiseptic mingling with the aroma of her apple blossom shampoo. "Can I take her home, Dr. Phillips?"

The older gentleman nodded. "I've written a couple of prescriptions for you two. But you both should be fine in a few days. If not," Dr. Phillips glanced toward Jorge, "I'd call your family physician."

Her family doctor and friend stepped forward. "I'll talk with Dr. Phillips. Right now, I think it would be a good idea to take Kaitlyn home. Do you need a ride? I can drive you."

"I'm taking them home," Daniel said, drawing her attention to the Ranger still at the end of the bed.

"I called him," she said in answer to the question in Jorge's eyes, purposefully not telling anyone who Daniel was. Although with his gun at his side and his silver star on his shirt, it was obvious he was a Texas Ranger.

"Fine. I'll call later to check up on you two. But don't hesitate to call if you have any problems."

"I won't." Melora assisted Kaitlyn to stand, her arm around her to steady her.

As she slowly walked her daughter from the room, Daniel came up to her side. "I'll bring my truck around to the entrance."

She tried to give him a smile, but her mouth wouldn't cooperate. She nodded instead.

After Daniel left, Jorge approached. "Are you sure there isn't anything I can do?"

"No, we're fine. But please don't say anything to my uncle. I didn't call him."

"Why?"

"I don't want to worry him."

"How do you know Ranger Riley?"

"How do you?"

"I saw him at Axle's funeral and asked Hank Zarvy."

"He's investigating Axle's murder."

Jorge stopped right outside the hospital's sliding glass doors. "And you called him?"

"Yes, I think this wreck is connected." At that moment Daniel pulled up and hopped out of his truck to help her and Kaitlyn get in.

Before she could climb in, Jorge stopped her. "What's going on?"

The worry in his expression battered at her composure. She didn't need to fall apart right now. Not with Kaitlyn looking to her for strength. "Don't worry. We'll be fine now that Ranger Riley is here."

* * *

As Daniel pulled up to her house, Melora caught sight of her uncle's restored 1956 Thunderbird and moaned.

"Who's visiting?" Daniel slowed his truck.

"Uncle Tyler. Jorge must have called him. I wish he hadn't."

"Uncle Tyler is here," Kaitlyn said from the backseat, excitement in her voice.

Melora glanced at her. "Yes. He's driving his latest toy."

Kaitlyn scrunched up her battle-scarred face. "Toy?" She sat up and looked out the front windshield. "Cool car and my favorite color—red."

"Yeah, Uncle Tyler's partial to red." A memory of Kaitlyn's face with bleeding cuts on it flooded her with fear all over again. Somehow she had to keep it from her uncle. She didn't want him pulled into her problems. She wasn't even sure what she was going to do—other than tell Daniel what was going on. She was in way over her head, fighting for her and Kaitlyn's lives.

A minute later when Melora let herself into her house, Uncle Tyler was striding across the large foyer toward her. She went into his embrace and battled to keep the tears that clogged her throat from spilling. Thankfully, at that moment Kaitlyn wedged herself between them.

He bent down and picked her up. "Hi, princess. I heard you had quite a day."

Although his voice was light and his expression showed only love for Kaitlyn, Melora glimpsed the tension in his eyes. She knew she would have some serious explaining to do—before she talked with Daniel.

"I was scared. Mommy and me were leaving on an adventure when that bad man hit us with a truck."

"What adventure?" Uncle Tyler swung his sharpened gaze to Melora.

"Don't know. It was a surprise." Kaitlyn threw her arms around her uncle's neck and kissed his cheek. "I'm glad to be home."

Juanita scurried into the foyer. "Oh, my baby, what happened to you?"

As Kaitlyn launched into an explanation about the wreck, Uncle Tyler's expression turned stony. There were only a few times when Melora had received that look—only when he was very displeased with her. She needed to talk with him before Kaitlyn said something about the cat disappearing. She didn't want the situation to get any worse than it already was.

Melora laid her hand on her daughter's back. "Juanita, I think Kaitlyn should have some of her favorite ice cream. That will make her feel better."

Daniel stepped forward. "That sounds great. Can I share some ice cream with you?"

"Yeah," Kaitlyn said. Her daughter took Daniel's hand and tugged him toward the kitchen.

Daniel was giving her the time to talk with her uncle, which she appreciated. Through all her dealings with Daniel lately, she realized one thing. He was a very perceptive man. Which meant she couldn't keep anything from him anymore. It took too much energy—energy she didn't have. But first she had to deal with Uncle Tyler.

"Let's go into Axle's office." A fitting place to have this conversation, she thought as she followed her uncle into the room and shut the door, preparing herself for the onslaught of questions.

"Are you really all right?"

His first query threw her off for a few seconds. She nodded.

"What were you doing in a cab?"

"How did you know about that?"

"I have connections. I checked with the police about the wreck. A hit and run."

"Yeah, the man fled the scene. Probably didn't have insurance."

"What's going on?"

Still achy and mentally exhausted, Melora crossed the office to a grouping of chairs and sat. "I was in a wreck. It happens. But I'm okay now and so is Kaitlyn."

Uncle Tyler took a seat across from her. "Why were you in a cab? What's this about an adventure?"

"With all that has happened lately, I thought it would be nice to get out of town for a while. Just Kaitlyn and me."

One of his bushy eyebrows rose. "Without telling me?"

"It was a spur of the moment decision. I was going to call you later."

"Is something going on you should let me know about? Why did you call Daniel Riley?"

"He's been looking into Axle's death, and we've renewed our acquaintance."

"I didn't realize you knew him."

"Casually. He's been working with the Alamo planning committee concerning the security."

Her uncle's gaze bore into her. "If something is wrong, you know I can protect you. You are my only family, Melora. You and Kaitlyn."

Love filled each of his words, and for a second she considered telling him everything. But looking into his dear features, she couldn't. Not yet. He'd given her a home when she'd lost her parents. He'd become like a father to her. She couldn't put him in the middle of this. She would never forgive herself if something happened to him because she'd involved him. Daniel was better equipped to protect her and Kaitlyn. She had to put her trust in him.

Melora pasted a smile on her mouth. "I love you, Uncle Tyler, and I'm going to be fine. Wrecks happen all the time in San Antonio. The police will find the driver." She hoped.

Two hours later in her living room Melora eased onto the couch, so tired all she wanted to do was stretch out and sleep like Kaitlyn was. After spending most of the previous night going over her plan to escape, Melora was exhausted both mentally and physically. Then her visit with her uncle had only added to that, but he'd left a half hour ago.

Daniel swiveled around from staring out the window that overlooked the several acres of backyard. His features firmed in a determined look, he moved toward the sitting area and took a wingback chair across from her.

"Thanks for waiting for your answers until Uncle Tyler left and I got Kaitlyn settled down for a nap. She went right to sleep." This time when she attempted to smile, the corners of her mouth lifted—slightly for a few seconds before collapsing.

"I'm glad. I was worried. She chattered for a while when she was eating her ice cream, then she became quiet. No amount of coaxing could get her to say much until you and Tyler came into the kitchen."

"Even then she was quieter than usual. I think everything was sinking in."

He removed his hat and placed it on the coffee table then lounged back. "Tell me what happened. Why were you in a cab?"

She prayed Daniel was the right person to trust. She looked him in the eye and before she lost her nerve said, "I was leaving San Antonio."

"Leaving? A vacation?"

"No, getting as far away from here as I could."

A shutter dropped into place over his expression. He straightened, leaning forward, his elbows on his thighs. "Why? Who has you scared?"

"I don't know who. The man who broke in was delivering a message to me to keep quiet or I would end up like Axle."

"Quiet about what?"

"That's just it. I don't know. He talked about a flash drive that Axle had, but I've looked in the house and can't find it."

Daniel clasped his hands together, his gaze zeroing in on her. "Do you think your husband was messed up in something illegal?"

The word yes stuck in her throat. She swallowed several times but still couldn't get it out. Finally she nodded, sliding her eyes closed. She didn't want to see the disappointment that she'd kept quiet for so long in his face.

The next thing she realized was that Daniel was

sitting down beside her on the couch, dangerously close, his lime-scented aftershave teasing her nostrils. "What did your husband do?"

"I don't know, but I think it involves his restaurants." She tilted her head around to peer at him, the dark orbs of his eyes mesmerizing. "When I became suspicious something wasn't right, I tried to discover what, but he found out and threatened me."

His expression softened. "Why do you think his restaurants were involved in something illegal?"

"I overheard him telling a man that nothing better go wrong with the shipment to the River-walk restaurant and that it better be turned around and out of there before the employees showed up the next day for work." She shuddered when she remembered Axle's lethal tone. "I'd never heard him talk like that."

"This man came to the house?"

"Yes. Axle wasn't too happy about that. The next time I saw the man was a week later. He and Axle were talking late one evening right before dark at the stable where we have a couple of horses. I never saw that man here again."

"Could you describe him for a sketch artist?"

"I could but I think it's the man who's been in a coma since September."

Daniel shot to his feet. "It is? Why didn't you come forward? The day of Captain Pike's murder, the man in the coma was found at the captain's house, shot and close to death himself. He may be the only one who can tell us what happened to Gregory, and we haven't been able to identify him." Anger slashed across his face as he glared down at her.

She opened her mouth to answer him when a scream curdled her blood.

SIX

"Kaitlyn!" Melora leaped to her feet and raced to her daughter's bedroom.

She heard Daniel right behind her. Silence came from Kaitlyn's room, which only heightened her fear. Had someone gotten to her?

It seemed to take forever to get to her daughter's doorway at the far end of the hallway on the second floor. Before she could charge into the bedroom, Daniel grabbed her arm and halted her.

"Let me," he whispered and withdrew his gun.

He peered inside, and the tension that gripped him melted as he holstered his weapon. Melora didn't wait for his go-ahead. She surged past him and hurried to Kaitlyn sitting straight up in her bed, tears coursing down her cheeks, her lower lip quivering.

"Honey, what's wrong?" She sat next to Kaitlyn and drew her against her.

"I dreamt…" The little girl swallowed the rest of her words and threw her arms around Melora.

"You're okay. I'm not going to let anything happen to you." Her daughter hugged her so tightly it was hard to breathe. Melora ran her hand down Kaitlyn's back over and over, trying to calm the fear the dream had unearthed. For the past few years she'd had her own share of nightmares.

When Kaitlyn leaned back several minutes later, her eyes still glistened with tears, but none ran down her face. She inhaled a deep breath and released it slowly. "Why did that bad man keep hitting our car?"

Melora combed her daughter's long hair back then cradled her head between her hands. "I don't know, but Ranger Riley is here to help me figure it out."

Daniel came to the bed and knelt near Kaitlyn. "I won't let anything happen to you and your mommy. We'll find the bad man."

"Promise?" Kaitlyn murmured, her arms still loosely about Melora.

He looked at Melora for a long moment then at Kaitlyn, a fierce resolve in his expression. "Promise."

In that second Melora knew she'd done the right thing by confiding in him. Staring at his commanding features, rugged, tan, she felt safe for the first time in years.

"Melora, is everything okay?" Juanita asked from the doorway.

With her coat still on, her housekeeper took a step into the room, clutching her purse and a small sack from the drugstore. Melora gave her a reassuring smile. "Yes, Kaitlyn had a bad dream and woke up scared."

Juanita's dark eyes clouded. "Do you need me to help with anything?"

"No, I know you have dinner to start. We're fine." *Or we will be when we find the person threatening us.* Again, another look at Daniel bolstered the feeling she'd done the right thing in telling him what was going on.

"Okay. Kaitlyn, there's some more of your favorite ice cream and I know how much you love it."

Her daughter's eyes bugged out. "Two bowls in one day?"

Juanita nodded. "If it's okay with your mom."

"Mommy, can I have some? I think it will make me feel better," Kaitlyn said in all seriousness.

The sight of her child's cuts hammered home how serious a situation they were in. She forced a light tone and a smile as she said, "Sure, honey. I need to talk with Ranger Riley."

Kaitlyn hopped off the bed. "Great."

Before she ran from the room, Melora added, "Don't forget to feed Patches in a little while."

"I won't," Kaitlyn said as she hurried out the door right behind Juanita.

"So strawberry ice cream will make things all

better with Kaitlyn. I wish real life was that easy."
Daniel moved closer to her. "Why didn't you come
forward when we splashed the sketch all over the
news asking if anyone knew the man's identity?"

Melora rose. "Because I'm not sure it is him and
I had other problems—like staying alive. The last
thing I wanted to do was talk to the authorities."

"Staying alive?"

"Yes. The break-in last week wasn't the first.
Right after my husband disappeared, there was
one. Two men wearing ski masks just like last
week. I was upstairs and had just finished putting
Kaitlyn down for the night after being at Uncle
Tyler's all day for Thanksgiving. I heard a noise
downstairs, and I knew it wasn't Juanita. She'd
gone to one of her sisters' for the long holiday
weekend." She glanced around at her child's possessions and realized this wasn't the place to tell
Daniel about what happened. "Let's go into Axle's
office. I wouldn't want Kaitlyn to overhear. She
doesn't know anything about this."

Melora left her daughter's bedroom and
descended the stairs. She hated moving to the
office, but it was the most private room and one
that Kaitlyn didn't come into much.

"Let me make sure she's okay in the kitchen
with Juanita." With a gesture toward the door to
the office, Melora strode to the kitchen and peered
in. Kaitlyn was helping Juanita put away some

groceries and telling her about what happened at the hospital. She backed away and headed for the meeting with Daniel.

Inside the office she found Daniel staring out the window. "I see the stable from here."

"Axle always liked to look out that window at the horses and stable. He loved to ride and planned to teach Kaitlyn when she was old enough." At one time she'd thought that at least Axle loved his daughter, but in the six months before he disappeared, she'd come to think that he'd only considered Kaitlyn another possession—one he'd used to threaten Melora with.

Daniel pivoted. "Is Kaitlyn okay?"

She nodded and took the chair nearest her. The emotional roller coaster she'd been on the past couple of days had caught up with her. And from the frown that settled on Daniel's face, she knew this meeting would be difficult at best.

He fit his long length into the chair across from her. "You were telling me about the first time your house was broken into. How did they get in?"

"I don't know. I suppose they could have come in when I took Kaitlyn up to her room. She'd fallen asleep in the car. I shut the door from the garage but didn't lock it. It took all I could do to turn the alarm off without waking Kaitlyn. She hadn't been sleeping well so I didn't want her to wake up."

"So you went downstairs to investigate a noise? You didn't call the police?"

"Truthfully, I wasn't really thinking. Like Kaitlyn, I hadn't been sleeping well, either. I thought it was Patches. He can get into things he shouldn't."

"So what happened when you confronted the two men?" Tension laced every word in Daniel's voice.

"I came into the office to find it trashed and one man standing by Axle's desk. The other was behind the door. I started to run out of the room when he caught me. I thought I was dead. Instead, they told me what they would do if I said anything to the police about the break-in or Axle. They made it very clear I would suffer the same fate as Axle if I didn't keep quiet and stay put in San Antonio."

"You mean to tell me that you knew Axle was dead and that something was going on with his business?" He gripped the arms of the chair. "If you had come forward two years ago, maybe Captain Pike wouldn't have been murdered."

His tightly spoken statement stunned her. For a moment she couldn't draw in a decent breath. Her lungs burned as did her thoughts. Had her silence caused Captain Pike to be murdered? What did Axle's death have to do with his? "That's a low blow." She bolted to her feet. "How can you say that?"

"Because somehow the captain's murder is tied to your husband's. I'm here to find the connection and the people responsible."

"I don't know anything about it. Axle has been gone for two years so he wasn't the one."

"You're involved somehow. There is a tie to both murders. Don't you want to find out who killed your husband?"

No, she wanted to shout. "They—the intruders from two years ago and the one last week—said I had more than myself to think about. That's all they needed to say to keep me quiet. I'm all Kaitlyn has. And I also have to consider Uncle Tyler who has done so much for me. I couldn't let anything happen to them."

"You said they were looking for a flash drive. Where is it?"

She rounded the back of the chair and clasped it, leaning against it. "I don't know. A few months before Axle went missing, he started wearing one around his neck. I guess that was the one they were looking for. I assumed it was on Axle when he was murdered. I told the men that."

"Nothing like that was found with the body. So either whoever killed him took the flash drive or he put it somewhere before he was murdered. Does your husband have a safety deposit box or something like that?"

"Yes and I checked it. Uncle Tyler and I went to

it to secure any papers for the business. Although my husband worked a lot from home, he did have an office at his corporate headquarters. I cleaned it out, too, and brought his personal items here." She waved at some boxes in the corner. "I left the business papers there for William Thompson."

"Could there be something in those that might help us?"

"I didn't see anything and my uncle looked over everything. He knows more about running a business than I do. Nothing seemed out of place."

"Would you allow us to look into the business and see if we can find anything?"

Once she said yes, she would be fully committing herself to this plan of action, which would put her and Kaitlyn in danger. But she already was a target. "Yes." She wanted this to end.

"Then I need to move on this right away. Can you call Mr. Thompson and tell him to cooperate fully with the Texas Rangers I'll be sending to his office?"

She nodded. "Are you going?"

"No. You trusted me with your secret even though it might put you and Kaitlyn in danger. I promised your daughter I would protect you two and I will. I'll be staying here until you're safe."

"Staying here?" she murmured, not sure how she felt about that. Part of her was comforted; another part was scared of the feelings he aroused in her.

She hadn't felt safe in a long time and with him she did. But it was more than feeling safe. It was a connection that went beyond his work.

"Yeah, and when I can't be here another Ranger will be. I'll call my office and send two Rangers to begin going through your husband's business today. I don't want to waste any more time or give anyone a chance to cover up something."

"I'll go check on Kaitlyn and make sure she's still all right and call William to tell him to expect some Rangers." She left the office and strode to the kitchen, withdrawing her cell as she walked.

At the kitchen entrance she spied Kaitlyn sitting at the table with a big bowl of ice cream, which would no doubt spoil her dinner, but she knew what Juanita was doing. Trying to get her daughter to forget about the wreck. She entered the room. "I see you're enjoying your ice cream."

With some on her upper lip, Kaitlyn nodded then spooned some more into her mouth.

"Juanita, Daniel will be staying for dinner."

A slight widening of her housekeeper's eyes was the only indication she was surprised. Since Axle's disappearance she had rarely entertained.

Kaitlyn bounced up and down in the chair and said, "Oh, goody. I'll get to show him Patches."

"Have you fed him?"

"Not yet. I will when I finish my ice cream."

Melora turned and strolled toward the large

picture window in the dining room and stared out front while she called William Thompson. When she informed the man of her wishes, she could hear the censure in his voice. "I must insist on this. Someone murdered my husband and needs to be found. Wouldn't you say so?"

"Well, yes, but—"

"Then we agree. There will be two Rangers showing up in a little while. Accommodate them any way you can."

After she hung up, she called the hospital, hoping that the cab driver was out of surgery by now. She had a friend on duty in the recovery room.

After learning the driver was in serious but stable condition, Melora slipped her cell into her pocket, thinking about the cab driver who had gotten caught up in what was happening to her. She couldn't let that happen to anyone else. Although she hadn't driven the truck that caused the wreck, she felt responsible. If she hadn't tried to run away, this might never have happened. She couldn't live like this anymore, and she hoped Daniel was the answer because she was placing her and Kaitlyn's lives in his hands.

Daniel let himself into his apartment and headed for his bedroom to pack a bag. With Gisella staying temporarily at Melora's, he would grab what he needed to stay indefinitely at her house. Both he and his captain felt she was a pivotal player in this case involving the Lions of Texas. That meant he had to keep her alive to help him get to the bottom of what was going on. Why had Axle been murdered? Who did it? What was Axle's connection to the Lions of Texas? Where was the flash drive? What was on it? Question after question tumbled through his thoughts.

Anderson and Oliver were at Axle's business, reviewing the business papers under the watchful eye of William Thompson. His own interview with Thompson a few days ago had proved fruitless, but maybe something would come of going through the paperwork at Hudson Restaurant, Inc. Ben had already heard from Tyler Madison demanding to know what was going on. His captain was fielding the man's inquiries, but threats to go to the governor were being tossed around.

When Tyler had called Melora, not two hours after his visit to his niece's, she'd been upset, telling her uncle that she needed to help with the investigation into Axle's murder. Her shaken demeanor after the phone call momentarily made Daniel forget that she'd kept quiet when she shouldn't have. In his job he lived with danger and fear. Melora didn't. He had to remember that. They needed to work together to find the connection between Axle's and Captain Pike's murders.

Daniel threw together the clothes and toiletries

he would need for a week, then glanced around to make sure he wasn't forgetting anything before making his way toward the door. A knock on it slowed his pace. He wasn't expecting anyone. Dropping his bag at his feet, he leaned forward and checked who it was through the peephole.

Clay. What was his son doing here? Then he remembered and groaned.

Pulling the door open, he stood to the side to let his seventeen-year-old into the house. "You're early."

"Basketball practice was over early so I came on over." Clay spotted the bag on the floor nearby. "Going somewhere?"

"I'm sorry I have to cancel tonight, but a case I'm working on—"

"Fine. It's not something that hasn't happened before." His son started to turn to leave.

"Hold it. Why don't you take the tickets to the Spurs' game and have a friend go with you? We can go to dinner and a game another night." Daniel withdrew his wallet and removed the two tickets he'd bought for a night with his son. He held them out to Clay, not sure by the frown on his face if his son would even take them.

Clay glared at them for a long moment, then snatched them from Daniel's grasp.

"If this wasn't important—"

"Dad, don't. I've heard that before. Thanks for the tickets." He pivoted and hurried out the door.

Daniel stared at the empty entrance. He'd done it again. He'd blown it with his son and he couldn't blame Clay for being upset. After three years of clashing over just about everything, he'd started making some headway with Clay recently and now this would set him back. If he didn't get so wrapped up in work, maybe he would have remembered about his plans with Clay and been able to make other arrangements.

With a heavy sigh, Daniel grabbed his bag and left his apartment. When this case was over, he would make it up to Clay somehow. Their relationship had always been rocky since Cheryl had divorced him when their son was four. She'd found another man who could give her what she wanted, and she'd made it clear to Clay it was his dad's fault their marriage had fallen apart. Cheryl had done everything she could to make sure her son didn't want to live with Daniel through the years.

Shaking those memories from his mind, Daniel reached his truck and slipped inside. He needed lessons on how to be a father. He certainly couldn't use his own sire as an example. He and his dad had butted heads most of their relationship. Like father, like son? He hoped not. He didn't want to make the same mistakes his father had with him, but it seemed as if he was heading down that path. Somehow he had to break the pattern.

When he parked behind Gisella's car in front of Melora's large house forty-five minutes later, darkness blanketed the landscape as though it were trying to cut them off from the rest of the world. Melora's place was in an area with few houses surrounding her. Each home in Lone Star Estates had several acres, which gave the impression of isolation.

Gisella opened the door for him.

"Any problems?" He entered the house, the scent of baking bread and roasted chicken peppering the air. His stomach rumbled its hunger.

Gisella chuckled. "Welcome to my world. I've smelled that for a couple of hours. And there weren't any problems other than my allergy to cats rearing its ugly head. It's been quiet except for Kaitlyn who let it spill that Patches had been missing for several days last week, then suddenly returned. The little girl thought they had lost him for good, but she'd been saying her prayers and God brought him back to her."

"Patches was missing? Melora didn't say anything about that." What else was she keeping from him?

"It's probably nothing, but you wanted to know if I learned anything out of the ordinary. Cats do tend to be independent and go off, but I didn't get the impression that Kaitlyn's had ever been gone overnight."

He removed his cowboy hat and tossed it on the table in the foyer. "Thanks. I'll check with Melora about it. She ran this morning for a reason."

"Kaitlyn is very attached to Patches. If something happened to the cat, that would certainly make a statement."

"And I intend to find out why someone is terrorizing Melora. What does she know about the flash drive?"

"She doesn't think she knows anything."

"Maybe she does but doesn't realize it. I'm taking her tomorrow to see the man in a coma at the hospital. She may have seen him meeting with her husband here at the house."

"That would be a break if we can find out more about him. See ya."

After Gisella left, Daniel was drawn toward the kitchen by the sounds coming from there. Leaving his bag in the foyer, he covered the distance to the room quickly, his appetite whetted by the aromas wafting to him.

Kaitlyn leaped to her feet when she saw him come into the kitchen. "You're here. We can eat now."

"You waited for me?" Daniel asked, realizing he and Melora had never talked about him eating dinner tonight with them. He'd even considered grabbing something on the way here, but for some reason he didn't stop, almost as if the aromas drew him across miles of San Antonio.

"We haven't been waiting long. I asked Gisella to stay if she wanted, but she had something she had to do tonight. If you've eaten, that's okay."

"Are you kidding? I haven't, and this smells wonderful."

Kaitlyn took his hand. "First, we've got to wash up. Mommy won't let me eat until I do. I'll show you where." Tugging on him, she led him toward the mudroom. "Mommy put a stepstool for me to use. One day I'll be tall like you and not use one."

While the child chattered about how important it was to sing the "Happy Birthday" song two times while washing her hands, Daniel stood there still slightly in shock, the words to the tune filling the air. Remembering his own son's childhood put Daniel on alert. He hadn't been very successful with Clay, and he was male. Daniel didn't know the first thing about a young girl.

Kaitlyn hopped down from the stool. "Your turn. Remember Happy Birthday," she held up two fingers, "two times."

"Sure," he murmured.

When he didn't start singing, Kaitlyn did. Halfway through the first time, he joined in, his voice strained. He said her name while she said Mr. Riley.

At the end she giggled. "Silly. This is your song."

"But it isn't my birthday."

"You have to pretend."

Pretending he knew how to do. For seventeen years he'd been pretending to be a father and not doing such a good job, according to both Cheryl and Clay. "I'll remember that next time."

Reentering the kitchen, he immediately captured Melora's attention and saw the twinkle in her eyes. Her mouth twitched as if she could barely contain her laughter. He could imagine how he sounded— off-key, stumbling over the words to a simple well-known song.

"It's been a while since I sang that," he said to her as he sat at the table set for three. "Juanita isn't joining us?"

"She's going out with a friend. She does most Mondays."

He lowered his voice and said, "So it isn't my presence that's keeping her away?"

"Don't flatter yourself."

"I understand, Juanita, you're leaving us to enjoy all this delicious food alone." Daniel gestured toward the table laden with a roasted chicken, cooked potatoes, carrots, onions and celery. "If I cooked all this, I wouldn't be able to resist sampling it. Must be an important person to keep you away…" he drew in a deep breath of the smells tempting him to salivate "…from this."

The housekeeper pinned her dark eyes on Daniel. "I've tasted my own cooking before." She untied an apron she had around her waist, slung it over the back of a chair and strode toward the hallway that led to her suite of rooms.

"She goes to see her older sister at Uncle Tyler's." Melora took her seat.

"Older sister?" Which one? When he investigated Juanita, he'd learned she had three.

"Carmen is Uncle Tyler's housekeeper."

"I see." He couldn't shake the feeling the reserved housekeeper wanted to avoid him. Why? Was it as Melora had said and Juanita didn't trust law enforcement or was it something else? The preliminary information Evan had found on the housekeeper didn't indicate anything that would make him think she was hiding something, but still the niggling sensation he'd learned to listen to plagued him when he was around the woman.

"C'mon, Mr. Riley. Mommy's waiting to say the blessing."

Daniel sat. "Just wondering if Juanita had a date."

"Like on TV?" Kaitlyn took a gulp of her milk, leaving a white mustache as evidence.

"Honey, remember the blessing. You need to wait."

The little girl leaned toward Daniel and whispered loud enough that Juanita could probably hear it in her room. "See what I mean?"

He winked at Kaitlyn, who had her mother's features but the coloring of her father. "Yes, I do."

Melora blessed the meal and not a second later Kaitlyn dived into her food as though she hadn't eaten in days. "We're not racing to see who is going to finish first, honey."

Kaitlyn paused shoveling in the vegetables and slowed her movements almost to a crawl—that lasted all of ten seconds.

Daniel kept his chuckle to himself, his gaze connecting with Melora's across the table. In that moment he felt her intense protectiveness toward her daughter, and he could begin to understand why she didn't know what to do when the threats started. He was exposed to evil in his job, but not Melora. She spent her time raising her daughter and volunteering to help others. Something inside him softened toward Melora as if he could place himself in her shoes and see where she was coming from. He did know he would do anything to protect Clay even if their relationship was rocky.

"It's been a long day, honey. It's time for you to get some sleep." Melora's body still ached from the wreck that morning. She covered Kaitlyn with the pink coverlet and bent down to kiss her.

Before she could, her daughter scooted up and sat back against the headboard. "How about a story?" She peered around Melora toward Daniel who stood in the entrance. "Will you read me one? Please, Mr. Riley."

"You don't want your mom to?" Daniel's surprised look encompassed his whole face.

Kaitlyn shook her head. "She can anytime."

"If it's okay with your mom."

Melora straightened and went to the bookcase, selecting the story that her daughter wanted to hear every night the past few weeks. Handing it to Daniel, she gave him a smile. "Go for it. If you can do voices, she loves that."

As Daniel took the book, Kaitlyn clapped her hands. "Yeah, Mommy does a great troll."

"I'll have to hear that one day." Daniel sat on the bed next to her daughter and opened the fairy-tale collection to the first story.

Kaitlyn splayed her fingers across the written page. "Not that one." After flipping through the book, she found the fairy tale she wanted and tapped it. "I want to hear Snow White. A prince saves her."

As Daniel began to read, Melora eased into the chair to listen to his deep, gruff Texas drawl. At first he was hesitant, but soon the words began to flow from him as he got into the story. By the end he even had the evil queen down with a wicked-sounding voice. Would he be her Prince Charming and save her and Kaitlyn? If he could, she was sure he would.

When he closed the book, Kaitlyn clapped. "Another one, Mr. Riley."

"Call me Daniel. We're gonna be spending a lot of time together. And as far as another story. Maybe tomorrow night."

Kaitlyn threw her arms around Daniel's neck and kissed him on the cheek. "Okay. You read better than Mommy."

Daniel's face reddened. He rose, peering back at Melora as though he didn't know what to say to her daughter.

Melora stepped forward. "Time for bed now."

As Kaitlyn snuggled down under the covers, Melora kissed her and switched off the bedside lamp with scenes of princesses from Disney movies.

"Good night, Mommy, Daniel."

In the dimness of the night-light, Melora made her way toward Daniel framed in the doorway, waiting for her. The soft look in his eyes hinted at a vulnerability that spoke to Melora. She'd known he had been married once and had a teenage son who lived with his mother. She couldn't imagine being separated from her daughter. That was the reason she'd stayed with Axle.

She closed her daughter's door partway then headed toward the kitchen. She still needed to clean up the rest of the dishes. If she kept herself occupied, maybe then she wouldn't focus on the pain she'd glimpsed in Daniel's eyes—as though he'd realized what he'd lost.

In the kitchen she began to rinse the plates to put in the dishwasher.

"Here, I can help you." Daniel came up and opened the appliance.

"You're a guest."

"A guest? Is that what I am?"

She slanted him a look and was captured anew by something in his eyes that spoke to her. Loneliness? She knew about that. "What do I call you then?"

"Until we find who killed your husband, I'm your bodyguard."

"What if we can't?"

"I will. If we discover what they want of Axle's, I have a feeling they will make themselves known to us."

"Can't I just wish them away?" Even she heard the weariness and fear in her voice. At least she didn't have to pretend anymore with Daniel that everything was all right when her life was falling apart.

He touched her arm, compelling her toward him. "They aren't going to go away until they get what they want or are caught."

"I know. This nightmare has to end now."

"Tell me about Patches."

"The cat? What do you want to know?"

Daniel released a long breath. "When are you going to trust me?"

SEVEN

"I'd say I'm trusting you with my life but even more so with my daughter's. Just by having you here, I'm taking a risk." Melora took a step back.

"If this is going to work, there can be no more secrets between us. Kaitlyn said something about Patches being gone."

Melora swung back toward the sink and turned on the water to continue rinsing the dishes. "Yeah, he disappeared for a while, but he's home. He's safe now." The fear she'd experienced at the time deluged her. Perspiration beaded her forehead, and her pulse sped just thinking about the incident and what happened because of it. She'd made a run for it, and she and Kaitlyn had ended up in an accident.

"There's more to it, isn't there?" He settled his hand on her shoulder, a gentle, supportive gesture.

She slid a glance toward him, and all tension was gone from his expression. Concern softened his eyes and beckoned her to let go of her fear and talk to him. "When you came over last week, that call I received was from someone letting me know if I didn't cooperate with them and keep my mouth shut, next time it would be Kaitlyn missing or me." She bit down on her lip to still the quaver in her voice.

His hand slipped from her shoulder to her arm, and he rotated her toward him. "Why didn't you tell me this sooner?"

"I am now. That was the reason I tried to run. And this morning I discovered I couldn't. They wouldn't let me."

"A direct threat against your daughter means we need to do things a little differently."

Her hands shaking, she stuck a plate under the flowing water then gave it to him. "What?"

"I'll have to make sure she is covered at all times. I don't want her to go to school. For the time being we'll keep her close to home."

"She'll want to know why. She loves school."

"Tell her she's taking her Christmas vacation a little early. Tell her whatever you need to." He cocked his head. "Anything else I should know?"

Tears blurred her vision. She kept her head turned away from Daniel. She felt her world falling apart. Her throat swelled. She would not cry in front of him.

"Melora, have you told me everything?"

His voice gently coaxed her. She wasn't alone anymore in this fight. Swallowing several times, she murmured, "I think so. I..." A glass slipped from her fingers and smashed against the granite sink.

Daniel reached around her and turned off the water then rotated her toward him. With his finger under her chin, he lifted her face and looked at her.

Through the sheen of tears she saw a smile brighten his eyes as they skimmed over her features. He cradled her face in his hands. "I know this isn't easy for you. I have a son, and if someone threatened him, I would do anything to protect him. You made the right decision to trust me." His voice was husky and warm.

"I shouldn't have tried to do this by myself, but I didn't know what to do. When I think about it, I don't understand any of this. I don't know anything other than Axle wasn't the man I married. He was fine until I questioned him about what he was doing. I'd heard him talking with that man who came to the house and I heard them mention drugs. I thought he was taking some kind of drug. That he might be sick and not telling me. Obviously, I'm naive about what is happening in the case." She laughed but heard no humor in the sound.

"Because you wanted to believe the best in your husband?"

She nodded. "When I asked him, he changed completely. Used Kaitlyn to keep me in line. When he disappeared, I thought he'd left me because our marriage had been rocky at best for the six months before he disappeared. I quickly realized that it wasn't Axle's style to walk away and leave everything. That's when I called the sheriff and reported him missing." She shuddered when she thought of that last encounter with Axle before she'd gone to the conference. His need to control her. Possess her like a trophy, not a person.

Daniel drew her to him and wound his arms around her. "I'm sorry you had to go through that. This is the first time you mentioned Axle talking about drugs. You may know more than you think once you let yourself remember."

The feel of his embrace gave her strength, pushed down the lump of emotion so she could lean back and stare into Daniel's eyes. "I want to box up everything in Axle's office. I think that's what we should do first. I've been through it, but maybe you'll find something I'm not seeing. My husband lived in a world I'm not familiar with."

"Then that's where we'll start looking, but first I want to take you to the hospital to look at the man in the coma. If it's the same person, you might remember something that can help us ID him. For months we've been trying to figure out who the man is. If we can ID him, we might be able to find out more to help us end what's been happening. Then I would like us to pay a visit to the Bustles and Spurs Café at the Riverwalk."

"Why?"

"Maybe there's someone at your husband's restaurant that you'll remember. You didn't see the man's face who broke in here, but you might remember his voice. I know it's a long shot, but it might pay off."

The same voice on the phone last week. Yes, she'd remember that. "How about Kaitlyn?"

"I'll have Gisella guard her. I already told her to be on standby in case I need a second person." He smoothed her hair back from her face and framed it between his large hands.

"Won't that let them know I've talked to you for sure?"

"After today at the hospital, I have a feeling they already know, and besides, now that you have, there isn't much they can do about it. Maybe then they'll leave you alone." He dropped his head toward hers.

His lips were inches away from hers, and they tingled with anticipation. In the middle of all that had happened, she wanted him to kiss her. She wanted to forget the past few weeks and become lost in his embrace.

At the last second he pulled back, his arms slipped from around her. She moved away, feeling as though she'd missed out on something worth a great deal.

He put more space between them. "I'd better go check and make sure the house is locked up tight."

She watched him hurry from the kitchen and couldn't shake the emptiness she experienced. Being so totally wrong about Axle caused her to be leery of men. Then why did she all of a sudden desire Daniel to kiss her?

In the dining room Daniel paused and gripped the back of a chair, leaning into it. What was he thinking? Kissing Melora? He knew all the reasons he shouldn't, but he couldn't get it out of his mind—the sight of her full lips waiting for his, her spicy scent spinning a web about him, the feel of her in his arms as though she belonged there.

His work was his life. He was good at his job and didn't need to be distracted by a beautiful, stately woman who was hurting. How could he heal her when he couldn't help himself?

A movement in the foyer riveted his attention. He straightened, his hand going to his holster.

Kaitlyn walked in, rubbing her eyes.

"What's wrong?"

"I heard a noise outside my window."

Melora gasped from the entrance into the kitchen.

He peered back at her. "I'll go check while you see to Kaitlyn."

"You're going outside?"

"Yes, but lock the door right after I leave and don't open it for anyone but me." He covered the distance to her. "And if I say everything is fine, don't open the door. Call the sheriff."

"But—"

"Do as I say," he whispered in a rough voice. "I'm going out the kitchen door. I'll come back to it when I need in. Okay?"

Eyes huge, Melora nodded and opened her arms for Kaitlyn to come to her. "Daniel will check to make sure there isn't anything out there that could get you." Hugging her daughter against her, she followed him to the back door.

Outside, he didn't move away until he heard the lock click in place. Then he withdrew his Wilson Combat pistol from his holster and gave himself a few minutes to let his eyes adjust to the darkness. Easing forward, he strode the perimeter of the house. Wind whipped by him. Clouds raced across the nearly full moon. The scent of rain hung in the air.

He rounded the corner of the house where Kaitlyn's room was. He didn't think it was anything since she was on the second floor, but he wasn't taking any chances with Kaitlyn or Melora. He slowed and scanned the area. With no bushes near, only a couple of leafless trees, he made his way to her window. A scratching sound like long fingernails against the glass filled the wind-tossed night. A tree branch scraped against the pane, which was probably what Kaitlyn heard.

But to be sure, he took his penlight from his pocket and checked the ground around the area below the window. Nothing.

Relief momentarily cloaked him, but quickly his usual vigilance pushed it away. The threat against Melora and Kaitlyn was still out there. Possibly watching the house right now. Again, he panned the area around him before heading back inside.

At the door he waited for Melora to open it, pleased she had followed what he'd said. "It wasn't anything. A tree branch against the window."

Melora breathed a sigh. "That's good."

"A tree branch," Kaitlyn said from the kitchen table, a glass of milk sitting in front of her. "Are ya sure?"

Daniel knelt in front of the little girl. "I will keep you safe."

Kaitlyn yawned.

"I know someone who is tired. Ready to go back to bed?" Melora came over to her daughter as Daniel rose, and held out her hand.

Kaitlyn peered up at both of them, her eyes

shiny with tears, her bottom lip trembling. "Do I hafta?" she asked, followed by another yawn.

"Yes." Melora slipped her hand around her daughter's and tugged her up. "But tell you what. I'll let you sleep in my room with me tonight."

"Thanks, Mommy." Kaitlyn threw her arms around Melora's waist. "How about Daniel?"

A bright cherry red painted Melora's cheeks. "He has his own room."

"Oh, okay." Kaitlyn started for the door, stopped and looked back. "C'mon."

"I'll walk you ladies to your room," Daniel said.

Kaitlyn hurried up the stairs ahead of them. "I left Mr. Snuggles in my room. I don't want anything to happen to him."

"Mr. Snuggles?" Daniel fell into step next to Melora, trailing several feet behind her daughter.

"Kaitlyn's stuffed dog. Axle wouldn't get another dog after his died two and a half years ago. Kaitlyn loved Bailey as much as Axle did. She used to snuggle up against him and fall asleep. He was so good with her even though she was a toddler. Last year when we were shopping, she saw the stuffed dog and thought it was her daddy's dog. I couldn't resist getting it for her."

"My son had a favorite stuffed monkey. He took it everywhere until it literally fell apart and his mother had to throw it away. He was mad at her for days."

Kaitlyn darted into her bedroom, snatched the brown stuffed animal off the bed and raced back into the foyer. "Mr. Snuggles was getting lonely."

At Melora's door, Kaitlyn went on into the room while Melora paused outside in the hallway and faced Daniel. "I'm glad you're here. I'm not sure what I would have done otherwise."

"I'm leaving my door open, and I'm a light sleeper. If you need me, all you have to do is yell."

She smiled, the sea green of her gaze sparkling like sun-bathed leaves.

The urge to kiss her drenched Daniel, but one look into her room put a halt to those thoughts. Kaitlyn lay curled on the top of the coverlet, her eyes drooping closed. "Good night."

Daniel waited until Melora went inside her bedroom and closed her door before pulling out his cell and calling Gisella. "I'll need you tomorrow to stay with Kaitlyn while I take Melora to see our coma guy. Melora told me tonight that someone called after the missing cat was returned and said her daughter was next if she talked," he said as he made his way downstairs.

"What time?"

"Ten. Then after we visit the hospital, I'm taking her to lunch."

"Lunch?" Surprise sounded in Gisella's voice.

"Don't get any ideas, Hernandez. We're going to Bustles and Spurs to see if she recognizes anyone at the restaurant."

"That could stir up a hornet's nest."

"Yeah, but we don't have much to go on right now except Melora and that someone thinks she knows where the flash drive is."

"What if that puts her in danger?"

The idea of Melora being in peril caused his fingers to clench around his cell as if he could pulverize it into dust. "She's already in danger. The only way to keep her safe is to find the person who murdered her husband and why. We need to find that flash drive and see why it's so important to others."

"See you tomorrow."

After he disconnected with Gisella, Daniel placed a call to his son to see how the game went. He wasn't sure Clay would even answer, but when he did, Daniel strained to hear Clay over the din. "Where are you?"

"At my buddies'."

"Doing what?" Daniel asked, and realized his mistake immediately.

"Nothing to concern you. I've got to go." His son clicked off.

Daniel brought his cell away from his ear and stared at it as though that would change the way the conversation had gone.

"Are you all right?"

He whirled around to find Melora standing in the entrance to the living room. "Just a little father/son bonding—not." He stuffed his cell back into his front pocket. "I wish I could go back and start all over...." He shook his head. "Never mind. That wouldn't change anything. I don't think I have what it takes to be a good father."

"Kaitlyn sure has responded to you. Not many people read her bedtime stories or get to have a detailed demonstration of how she takes care of Patches."

"That's because I was here."

Melora glided forward. "Exactly. Being around someone is important."

"Yeah, I know and I haven't done a good enough job in that department with my son. My job demands most of my time, and I have an ex-wife who has tried everything to keep me and Clay apart. Soon he stopped wanting to do much with me. I think he thought it was easier than making his mother upset. I didn't want him to feel he was the rope in a tug-of-war contest."

"It's tough when parents put a child in the middle. Divorce is hard enough on a child without being the prize in some kind of fight between the parents."

"I know. I couldn't do that to Clay."

"So you backed off?"

"Not totally. But as he was growing up, every time I couldn't make it, Cheryl made it into a big deal with Clay to the point he stopped wanting to do things with me. About the only time I felt needed in my son's life was when he got into trouble with the local police. He was fourteen and joyriding in a car an older boy had stolen. Clay said he didn't know it was stolen. He thought it was Brad's. The officer took him, along with the other three boys, to the station. He called Clay's mother then me since he knew me. When I came to the station, I'd never seen my son so scared. When he was given community service, he got upset with me for not using my connections to make everything go away. Our relationship hadn't been very good before that. Afterward it nosedived. Only recently have we begun doing things again."

"But you were there for Clay when he was in trouble. That has to count for something."

His role model hadn't been the best. His dad had wanted him to do things his way to the point that the last years he was alive they'd hardly talked. No matter what Daniel did, he seemed to repeat the same mistakes his own dad had made with him. "So what do you recommend I do to make things better between Clay and me?"

"Spend time together—quality over quantity."

"I was supposed to go to a Spurs game tonight,

but I had to cancel. I gave him my ticket to take a friend."

"But that isn't the same thing as spending time with him. I'm sorry you had to cancel because of me."

The genuine concern in her voice prompted him to close the space between them. "It isn't your fault. This is my job. Things come up that have to be dealt with right away. The problems between Clay and me go much deeper than not spending time with him because of my job." How did he tell her every time he was with his son he found himself going into protective mode—dictating what he thought was best for Clay?

"But still, your son is important to you." She looked away for a moment then reconnected eye contact. "Even with Kaitlyn at her age, I've found listening to her concerns is one of the best ways to connect with her. Clay is going to graduate from high school soon. What does he want to do after that?"

"I hope he goes to college and—"

She placed her warm fingers over his mouth. "What does Clay want, not you?"

For several heartbeats he could only think about her fingers on his mouth, her beautiful eyes peering at him, her fragrance driving all other scents away. He captured her hand touching him and held it for a few seconds against his lips before cupping it between his two palms. "He loves to play basketball. A couple of years back all he wanted to do was become a pro basketball player." Reluctantly, he released her.

"What now?"

"He hasn't said too much to me about what he wants to do in the future."

"Why not?"

Daniel thought back to the conversation when Clay had informed him he was going to play professionally and his reaction. He'd told him all the reasons that wasn't a good game plan for his future. "Probably because I didn't encourage him."

"How old is he? Sixteen, seventeen?"

"Seventeen."

"Sometimes we have to let our children go and try things on their own."

"But what if we don't think it's a good idea?"

"Be there to listen and support, but unless it's something like falling into a life of crime or hurting himself or others, sometimes a kid has to figure things out for himself."

Daniel kneaded the tight cords of his neck. "I'm doing exactly what my father did. I wanted to go into law enforcement. He wanted me to go into his business. We parted ways over that. Our relationship got rockier because he wouldn't listen to me."

"Then I think you know what you need to do."

She made it sound so simple. He had his doubts, but he and Clay needed to have a heart-to-heart over his future plans. "I thought you were going to bed."

"I am. I forgot the book I was reading. It helps me to fall asleep."

"Must not be a very good story." Staring into the liquid green of her eyes made him want to melt against her and ravish her mouth. He backed away. These feelings were just because she'd listened to him. Nothing more, and he needed to remember that.

Chuckling, she started across the foyer. "It serves its purpose. I left it in the kitchen. Good night."

"See you in the morning. I'll check the house one last time and then I'm going to bed myself." He followed her into the kitchen and went to the back door to make sure it was secured.

At the bay window in the breakfast nook, he peeked outside. As Melora left the room, he wondered if someone was out there watching the house, waiting to make his move. They needed to get a break on this case soon, he thought, turning away and continuing his rounds.

Melora should be used to the smells in a hospital since she volunteered at least once a week at Mercy, but every time she came she was reminded of her parents' deaths. A car out of control had skidded over the sidewalk and crashed into an outdoor café where her mother and father were having lunch. Her dad had died on the way to the hospital, her mom a little later in the emergency room.

When she'd first started volunteering in the gift shop at Mercy, she'd forced herself to stay each day, fighting nausea at the aromas that vividly brought her back to that time in her life. Now she was used to it—mostly. Her stomach still clenched momentarily when she stepped through the hospital entrance.

"Okay?" Daniel took her elbow and guided her toward the elevator. "This shouldn't take too long."

"Hospitals remind me of my parents' deaths. I'll be fine in no time."

"And you volunteer here? How do you do it?" He allowed her to step on to the elevator first.

"I'm not going to let something like that stop me from helping people. Besides, I don't like my past dictating what I do now. I've had enough of that."

"Sometimes easier said than done."

The ding signaled that they had arrived at their floor, and the doors swished open. The antiseptic smell was stronger up here than in the lobby. Her stomach gurgled. "You sound like a man dealing with his own past."

He marched toward a room halfway down the

hall. "I think everyone has to deal with the past at some time. As you know, mine is my son." Daniel nodded to Evan on duty inside the patient's room. "How is he today?"

The Ranger angled away from the TV monitor which displayed the hospital corridor outside the door. "He's moved some this morning. The doctor was here earlier and is hopeful that he'll wake up soon."

"That's good news we can use. As I told you this morning, I brought Melora to see if she can ID him."

Melora ignored the two Rangers talking and focused on the man in the bed. His pasty features weren't the tan ones she'd remembered, but he'd been in a coma for months. The strong jawline, the brown hair, longer than she recalled but the same medium shade, the scar under his left eye all attested to the man who visited Axle on several occasions two years ago. A man who had scared her with the cold look in his eyes. Was that why she'd eavesdropped on his conversation with Axle?

"That's the man I saw at our house with Axle. The first time he came they argued. That's the only time I heard Axle call him Quin when they came to an agreement and my husband patted him on the back as if he were his best friend."

"No other name?" Daniel joined her at the side of the bed.

She shook her head. "And I couldn't tell you for sure that Quin was his first or last name, but I got the impression it was his first name."

"What did he sound like?"

"He had an Irish accent."

"That confirms what we heard from a tip we received." Daniel looked at her. "What about the second time this man came to the house?"

"When Quin came again to see Axle, they met at the stable."

"Did they go anywhere special?"

She thought back to that last time she saw the man in the coma, trying to remember where they had gone. "Besides the stable, they circled around the back of the property. That's all I saw."

"Okay. We have a bit more that might help in narrowing down who this man is. Let's grab something to eat at the Bustles and Spurs Café." Daniel nodded to the other Ranger. "Thanks, Evan. If anything changes with him," he gestured toward Quin, "let me know. I'll call headquarters about what we found out today."

Out in the hallway, people went about their daily tasks while Melora felt her life was coming apart, one thread at a time. Was the fact she'd known one of the man's names enough to help end this nightmare? Probably not, but finding what the people wanted of Axle's might.

"When we get home, I want to start looking in Axle's office right away."

"Do you want to eat at the Bustles and Spurs or somewhere else?"

She wanted to limit the places she went but didn't want to spend too much time at the Bustles and Spurs, not after what she was discovering about the restaurant chain her husband owned. "The restaurant here at the hospital has great food. I've often gotten lunch there when I volunteer."

Back by the elevator, Daniel pressed the button for the ground floor. Five minutes later they entered the café attached to the hospital. After finding a table in the corner, Melora spotted Jorge sitting nearby with two other doctors, finishing up their meal.

Daniel scanned the restaurant. "It looks like a lot of the staff comes here."

"Yeah, the service is fast and the selection of food is a little different from the cafeteria. It gives an alternative for people who are visiting the hospital but especially for the staff."

After ordering, Melora tried to relax back in her chair, but tension coated every nerve with a hard outer shell. "Will what I told you help in any way?" Since she'd made the decision to aid the Texas Rangers, she desperately needed to know that had been the right move to make.

Daniel shrugged. "It's another piece of the

puzzle. We need to ID the man and now we not only know he's Irish but one of his names is Quin."

"What if that is an alias?"

"It still might help us." He leaned forward as though trying to get as close to her as possible with a table for four between them. "What I think would really help the case and you is finding what Axle had that everyone is interested in getting their hands on, so I agree that's what we need to focus on now."

Jorge Cantana threaded his way through the crowded tables and stopped near Melora. "Are you and Kaitlyn all right? I didn't hear anything from you, so I guessed you were. I didn't want to disturb you if you were resting."

"I'm sorry, I should have called you. Both Kaitlyn and I are sore, but that is to be expected after being in a car wreck." She drilled her gaze into Jorge. "Why did you tell Uncle Tyler about the accident?"

His eyebrows beetled together. "I didn't. You asked me not to."

"You didn't?" Then who did? Probably someone else at the hospital. Her uncle was on the board so a lot of people knew him there. She would call her uncle and find out when he came back from his business trip.

"No. I thought you might like to know the cab

driver is awake and out of danger." Jorge smiled at Melora then turned his attention to Daniel. "Is something wrong? Why are the Texas Rangers interested in a car wreck?"

"We aren't usually."

Jorge opened his mouth to say something else, looked at Daniel and then peered at Melora. "If you are in trouble, I'll help any way I can."

"Melora and I are friends. I've known her for years. Since her husband's body was finally uncovered, we've been getting reacquainted." Daniel placed his hand over hers on the table.

To cover her surprise at Daniel's words, Melora gave Jorge a grin, but the tension at the table heightened with each second he remained. She'd noticed Daniel hadn't revealed much to Jorge, and she could understand his caution. The less people knew the better, even a friend of the family. But to give the impression they were dating had come as a shock. "I'm fine. I hope we can get the girls together soon."

"Just call to set up a play date."

"With the holidays, things are hectic."

"I know what you mean. We're going out tonight to shop for Cara. See you, Melora. Remember Beth and I are only a phone call away." Jorge nodded toward Daniel before leaving.

"Is he a good friend?"

"He's the family doctor, and I'm friends with his

wife. Our daughters play together. They don't live too far from me. After Axle disappeared, Beth and Jorge were there for me."

"I got the distinct impression he didn't like not knowing what's going on."

Melora chuckled. "That's Jorge. Beth accuses him of sticking his nose in every place he can. I think that's what makes him such a good doctor, though. He's very inquisitive and curious. His patients rave about how he'll keep digging until he finds out the answer to a problem."

"I don't have to tell you to keep quiet about what I'm really doing. People can wonder, but they don't have to know for sure. Let them think there's something between us. Keep them guessing."

His hand still covered hers. Heat scored her cheeks as she slipped hers into her lap. She'd seen the questions behind Jorge's congenial expression. When it became known that Daniel was staying at the house… Melora stared at her plate. She was glad that her uncle was out of town for a few days. He would demand answers to some very personal questions, and she wouldn't lie to him.

Returning to the Bustles and Spurs on the River-walk brought back memories of her marriage with Axle—not all bad, at least not at first. But over the years something had changed with Axle. He became driven. Getting more money had become

She smiled up at him. "He's wearing jeans and a brown shirt and cowboy hat."

Daniel pulled her even closer, his expression intense as if she were the most important person to him. Her heart reacted to his nearness and the threat that loomed on the bridge.

Casually, they began strolling toward the left. "I see him. Medium height, the same build as your assailant."

"The same man?" She hadn't thought about that. She swung her gaze toward the young man again as he flicked his cigarette into the water below.

He straightened from the railing, spun on his heel and darted down the other side of the bridge. Daniel took a few steps forward to go after him but stopped and twisted back toward Melora.

"Why didn't you go after him?"

"Because my job right now is to keep you safe. What if someone had set this all up to get me to do just that?"

An icy shroud wrapped about her. She surveyed the area and wondered who else was watching.

EIGHT

Later that day, Melora placed another drawer full of Axle's belongings into a box then marked what was in the container as she sealed it. "Do you think that sketch I gave of the young man will help you all?"

Daniel started on a new row of books on the shelves. "I didn't get that good a look at his face, but what you told the sketch artist was what I saw."

"The problem was his face was not totally visible today, and the last time I saw him he was a distance away."

"All we can do is run with what we have and hope something happens. That man might be the same one who broke into your house so he's definitely a person of interest."

And he was watching her. If she heard him talk, she could identify him for sure, but right now she needed to focus on finding Axle's flash drive—if it even was here at the estate. "That's it for the desk.

It's cleaned out and no flash drive. In fact, nothing that remotely looks like information someone would murder to get." She was still afraid that Alicia Wells would be found dead. Although it appeared the woman had betrayed Melora, she didn't want her killed for it.

"When we're through in here, we'll at least be able to rule out this room." Daniel took another book from a shelf, flipped through it then put it into a carton.

Melora sat back in the desk chair, tired from spending all afternoon working on boxing up Axle's possessions while searching for the elusive flash drive that Daniel hoped would lead to who was behind his captain's murder. Going through her deceased husband's belongings brought forward all those memories she wanted to forget and move past.

Daniel completed going through the shelf of books, ones that Axle had loved to read about war and violence, and closed the carton. Melora wished she could shut the door on her past as easily as it was to box up Axle's possessions.

"After we finish up in here tomorrow morning, where do you think we should look next?" Daniel walked to the desk and hovered over her.

His presence gave her comfort. For a few moments she felt safe, protected. Then she glanced at the stacked containers along the wall and knew she wasn't safe. "His bedroom. We slept in separate ones those last six months." Admitting the failure of her marriage out loud didn't bother her as much as it would have a month ago. But she couldn't shake the feeling that Axle had fooled her for years. Why hadn't she seen what kind of man he really was?

He held out his hand to her. "C'mon. We deserve a break. I've been smelling dinner for the past hour."

She allowed him to tug her up, the feel of his touch zipping up her arm and through her body. "Juanita is fixing her Mexican casserole. It's delicious."

"I haven't had anything she's made that isn't wonderful. I just wish she would relax around me."

She should move away from him, put the room between them, but Melora stayed rooted to the floor right in front of Daniel. His dark eyes lured her in, tying her to him. "She's that way around most new people. It takes a while for her to warm up. It took her a year with Axle."

Still clasping her hand, he inched closer. "A year! Let's hope I'm gone by then."

He said it lightly, referring to his investigation, but his words reminded her that their "partnership" was short-lived. She stepped back to reinforce that.

"This case has lasted long enough. I don't want you living in fear," he said in a husky drawl that enticed her to come nearer.

"Mommy. Daniel. I've drawn you a picture." Kaitlyn rushed across the room, waving two sheets of paper.

Melora scrambled back, nearly collapsing into the desk chair behind her, while Daniel whirled around and held out his hand for his drawing.

He took the paper Kaitlyn thrust at him and grinned. "This is beautiful. You're gonna be the next Picasso."

Kaitlyn's forehead wrinkled. "Pisa—so? Who's that?"

Melora skirted around Daniel. "A famous painter. Let me see."

Kaitlyn gave Melora her sheet.

"I love dogs. I used to have a brown one like this," Daniel said.

The little girl giggled. "That's not a dog, silly. It's a horse. Like the one in the stable."

"Oh, now I can tell." Daniel turned a nice shade of red and threw Melora a "help me" look.

"This will be perfect up on the refrigerator." Melora drew Kaitlyn to her and kissed the top of her head. "Thanks, hon."

"Can we show Daniel the stable?"

Melora looked toward him, not sure how to answer.

He drew in a deep breath. "I smell dinner and my stomach has been rumbling for hours."

"We'll take Daniel to the stable another day. Go wash up for dinner."

Kaitlyn spun around and raced from the room. "I'll draw him a picture of the stable then."

"That whirlwind was my daughter just in case you couldn't tell."

Daniel chuckled. "I haven't had someone draw me a picture in—" he cocked his head and thought "—come to think of it, never."

"She loves to make pictures. I have a whole scrapbook of them. I put them up on the refrigerator for a while then they go into the scrapbook. Something for me to look back over in my old age."

"I wish I had something like that with Clay. If only I could have do overs—with my son and father."

Melora responded to the sadness flashing into his eyes and laid her hand on his arm. "We can't exactly, but we do get second chances. Think of tonight as one of those."

Their gazes connected, and she wanted to help erase the vulnerability she saw in his expression. She moved closer. "I know your dad is dead, but what's stopping you from asking your father to forgive you now? It's how you feel that is important. If you regret what happened to your relationship with your father, then ask his forgiveness then move on. That's all you can do."

Juanita appeared in the dining room doorway. "Melora, do you want to eat in the dining room or kitchen?"

"Kitchen will be fine. I'll be in there to set the table."

"Kaitlyn is spread out all over the table, drawing a picture for Señor Riley."

"We can wait until after Kaitlyn finishes her picture, then eat. I know you're planning on going to church tonight. Go ahead and I'll take care of whatever else needs to be done."

"If you're sure."

"I am." Melora waited until Juanita left before continuing, "She usually takes this evening totally off, but since you're here, she offered to stay and fix dinner. I accepted when I thought of my cooking versus hers. There is no comparison."

"She goes to church every Tuesday night?"

"Yes."

"Which church does she go to?"

"Lone Star Christian. Why?"

He shrugged. "Just curious." He started for the kitchen.

Melora grabbed his arm and halted his progress. "Are you going to check up on Juanita?"

His stare, as though they had never talked about

personal issues just minutes before, drilled into her. "I already have some."

"Juanita is like a member of my family. She would never do anything to harm me or Kaitlyn."

"Often murders are committed by friends or loved ones so excuse me if I don't take that as a reason not to look closely into Juanita's activities." His professional facade firmly in place, he shook off her grasp and continued his trek toward the kitchen.

Was he regretting their earlier connection? There was a part of her that saw the wisdom in that. But a small piece of her clung to that link she'd experienced with Daniel for a short time this evening. She'd felt as if her opinion mattered, something that had been lacking in her marriage.

Later that evening, Melora entered the third floor circular tower, darkness beyond the large windows that, in daylight, afforded her a view of the surrounding landscape. But rays of moonlight streaked across the wooden floor, illuminating her way toward Daniel. "There you are."

He stood at the west window that faced the front of the house, his hands stuffed into his jeans, his shoulders hunched. "I came up here to check the door to the deck. Although not the most likely way for someone to get into your home, it could happen." He turned from the window and faced her. "I like it up here."

"It's my favorite room in the house. I've done a lot of thinking up here. I could look out and feel as though I was on top of the world while I wasn't."

He closed the space between them. "I'm sorry for all that's happened to you."

"I just want my daughter safe. I want a normal life again. I haven't had one in years."

"Normal? What's that?"

"I noticed you were awfully quiet tonight at dinner and afterward. Did Kaitlyn nagging to play a game bother you?"

He shook his head. "On the contrary, I enjoyed playing Candy Land."

Melora laughed. "That's a first. I don't think I've heard that from a man. Axle never…"

"I'm not Axle." The words were bitten out between clenched teeth.

She didn't want to talk about her deceased husband, she suddenly thought. She wanted to put that part of her life behind her. How was that possible with all that was going on right now? "I know, but she could never get Uncle Tyler, either." She forced a lightness to her voice. "And believe me, she tried some of her best whining with Uncle Tyler."

"I have succumbed to your daughter's vast charms."

"How about her mother's?" The question came

out in a breathless rush that sent her heart hammering against her rib cage.

His mouth spread in a smile. "From the first time I came to your rescue."

She shivered. "I hate to think what would have happened if you hadn't."

He took her hand, brought it to his lips and kissed her palm. "No matter where we are, I'll do my best to protect you."

"I know because that's the type of man you are." Nothing like Axle.

He leaned toward her and brushed his lips across hers before settling his mouth on hers in a deep kiss. She melted against him as though her legs couldn't support her anymore. His arms held her to him while he continued to lay claim to her heart. When he finally lifted his head, his embrace still caged her against him.

"I shouldn't have done that," he murmured in a husky voice that renewed all those tingling sensations his kiss had generated.

"Probably not." Melora circled her arms around his neck.

"We need to keep this business between us."

"Yeah, I'm sure you're right." She dragged him down for another kiss. It had been years since she'd felt this cherished. Actually, it had been never. Certainly not with Axle.

He murmured something against her lips, but

this time she was the one who initiated the deepening of the kiss. With all that happened to her in the past few years, she wanted—needed—this feeling of femininity—of closeness.

When they parted, their shallow breaths filling the void between them, Melora finally let her arms slip to her sides and took a step back.

In the sliver of light Daniel's expression, full of his own needs and wants, transformed into a neutral one. "We'd better call it an evening. Tomorrow we have a lot of house to cover."

Stepping another pace away from him, Melora nodded, not even sure if he saw the gesture as she let the shadows swallow her up.

He cleared his throat. "We'll finish the office then start on your husband's bedroom."

Another room she avoided when she could. Axle kept the master bedroom downstairs while she'd moved to the second floor to the room next to Kaitlyn's. Even from the grave he was influencing her actions.

Now that she was no longer in Daniel's embrace, she saw the folly in getting involved with him. They had come from the same world, but he'd left it behind. His work was his life—like Axle. At least Daniel was on the side of good, but at one time she had thought Axle was a good guy, too. And she had been very wrong. Could she ever risk falling in love with another man? That mistake with Axle could cost her her life—or her daughter.

After escorting Melora to her room, Daniel made another round to check the doors and windows. His body felt charged, restless. He shouldn't have kissed her, but the connection he sensed with her overwhelmed him. He'd been able to talk to her as though they had known each other for years. She'd tried to make him feel better about his relationship with his son.

But the fact his relationship was so rocky with Clay was the very reason he needed to stay away emotionally from Melora—and as far from her as possible physically when she was safe again. He needed to keep reminding himself that she deserved a man who could give her one hundred percent. She deserved a man who could be a good father to her child. That wasn't him.

The kiss was nice. No, it was great. But that was all they would share. He was here for two things— to protect her and Kaitlyn and to find Axle's flash drive. Nothing else.

Kaitlyn raced into the office as Daniel finished taping up the last box. "Mommy just told me you wanted to play another game of Candy Land tonight." The little girl threw her arms around Daniel's waist and hugged him.

Surprised, he looked up to see Melora entering the room. "You've gotta give a guy a rematch."

Her daughter had a way of overwhelming a person and the expression on Daniel's face illustrated that right now. Melora slid her look away, taking in the almost empty room, void of most of its personal touches. "That's only if you pick up your room."

"Ah, Mommy." A pout puckered her mouth. "I'll just mess it up again." Kaitlyn leaned back and stared up at Daniel. "Don't ya think so?"

"Well…" He sent a "please help me" glance toward Melora.

"Honey, your room first, then later a game of Candy Land. Daniel and I need to finish cleaning up in here and putting Daddy's things away in his room."

Kaitlyn whirled around and faced her mother, her hand on her waist. "What are you gonna do with his stuff?"

Melora walked to her daughter, a smile spreading across her features. "I'm saving them for you. When you get older, you can decide what we do with them. Okay?"

"Okay." Kaitlyn hurried from the office.

Daniel wiped his brow. "Whew! There for a

moment I thought you were going to have a fight on your hands."

"Kaitlyn hasn't said too much about her daddy being gone. He wasn't around that much. When he was home, he usually holed himself up in here and didn't see her a lot."

"So work consumed him, too."

"Not so much work as his life. Axle did what he wanted to do. Nothing more than that. Sometimes it was work. Sometimes it was play. We were an aside to him."

With three strides, he cut the distance between them. "I'm sorry."

"You aren't like him," she said in a voice that made him wonder if she was trying to convince herself or him.

"Are you sure about that?"

"Yes." Her voice was fierce.

Neither said or did a thing for a good minute until the doorbell's chimes sliced the tension in the air.

Melora pivoted and started for the door. Daniel snagged her arm and stopped her progress.

"Let me answer it." Steel threaded through his words. He didn't like the picture of himself materializing in his mind—someone like her deceased husband who neglected his family and did what he wanted.

Melora stood back a few feet while Daniel

checked who was at the door then opened it. Her uncle filled the entrance into her house. His expression, full of worry, froze her. She'd never seen such concern in his eyes as she did today. Something was terribly wrong.

"What's the matter, Uncle Tyler?" She finally moved forward. Even at her parents' funeral he'd been in control of his emotions. Now she sensed he barely had them reined in.

"We need to talk." Her uncle stabbed Daniel with a hard look. "Alone."

Daniel closed the door. "I'll be in the kitchen trying to get one of those cookies I smell baking."

After he left the foyer, Uncle Tyler strode to the office and went into the room, only to come to a halt a few feet inside. "What have you been doing?"

Melora came up behind him. "Boxing up all of Axle's possessions. I thought it was about time."

"What are you going to do with them?"

"Store them somewhere. I hadn't thought that far ahead."

The frown she used to dread carved his features. "Obviously, you haven't. What is a Texas Ranger doing here? I leave town for a couple of days and you two have become inseparable." He paced toward the window and looked out to the stable. "Why?"

She hadn't wanted her uncle to be dragged into what was going wrong with her life, but she had to tell him something. She moved toward him. "He's protecting me."

He swept around. "From who?"

She lifted her shoulders in a shrug. "Someone broke into my house last week."

"And that warrants the attention of a Texas Ranger?" He shook his head as though ridding his mind of some unwanted thoughts.

"Axle was into some illegal activities that they are interested in."

Uncle Tyler stepped closer. "I can hire body-guards—a whole army of them—if you want. Let me protect you. Please stop what you're doing before something happens to you or Kaitlyn."

The vehemence in his voice stole her words. She stared at him for a long moment before finally asking, "Has someone threatened you?"

"It's not me I'm worried about. It's you. I can't protect you anymore. I've tried since Axle's death."

"What are you talking about?"

His tanned features drained of all color at the same time as a thud resonated through the office. When he opened his mouth to reply, Uncle Tyler's eyes going wide froze Melora for a few seconds. A bright spot of red on his chest fanned outward as he crumbled to the floor.

NINE

Melora opened her mouth, but no sound came from her throat. Finally, her muscles began to work, and she knelt next to her uncle. With trembling hands, she reached toward him. His eyelids fluttered, then he looked right at her.

"I'm sorry. If we could—have found the…" he rasped, the light fading from his eyes as they stared at her.

A scream erupted from deep inside her. Seconds later, Daniel slammed the door wide and rushed into the room, his gun drawn. With a quick visual sweep, he assessed the situation, holstered his weapon and hurried toward her.

"Are you all right?" he asked as he stooped to feel for Uncle Tyler's pulse at his neck, then closed the older man's eyes.

Tears blurred Melora's vision while she stared at her uncle, blood pooling on the floor about him. Everything inside her iced. He'd raised her. Now he was gone, too. Because of her.

Vaguely she saw Daniel check the window with a bullet hole in it, then shut the drapes. Then he placed a call about the shooting, but his words jumbled around in her brain, making no sense. Nothing made sense. More tears flooded her eyes and rolled down her cheeks as hands lifted her from the floor and wrapped about her. The quaking began and quickly spread to envelop her.

"We were…" she gasped in a shallow breath "…he just went down."

Holding her to him, Daniel guided her from the room into the foyer and sat her on the bottom stair, then went down on his haunches in front of her, grasping her elbows. "Are you hurt anywhere?"

His gaze skimmed over her, and she peered down to see what he was looking at. Blood drops splattered her snowy white blouse. She fixed on some right above her heart, pain, not from a bullet, lanced through it. Her throat crammed with the tears she tried to keep in, she shook her head.

"Where's Kaitlyn?" she asked, locking gazes with him.

"She was in the kitchen with us. I had Juanita take her back to her room and told her not to come out until I told her to."

She lifted her quivering hand and pointed toward the office. "He's dead because of me. They want me, not Uncle Tyler."

"What did he want to talk to you about?"

Melora swallowed several times, trying to think back five minutes to what Uncle Tyler had been saying to her. For a few seconds her mind blanked, except for the vision of her uncle right before he collapsed to the floor. Surprise then fear flashed across his face. "He was telling me he could protect me. He was worried about me." She tapped herself on the chest. "Me, Daniel, and he's the one dead. It should have been me."

"Did he say anything else?"

The tears returned when she remembered her uncle's last words. "He was telling me he was sorry. He had nothing to be sorry about. He raised me when my parents died. He didn't have to. I'm the one who is sorry for pulling him into this." She pushed to her feet. "I need to see Kaitlyn. Make sure she's okay."

He settled his hands on her shoulders, keeping her in front of him. "You need to change first and wash up."

Another glance at the blood sent numbing waves through her. *Lord, how am I supposed to deal with all this? Please. I need You.*

Then she noticed the blood on Daniel's light blue shirt. She gestured toward it. "I'm sorry," she murmured the same words her uncle had told her.

Sobs overwhelmed her, and she went into Daniel's arms again, seeking some kind of solace, something to take this pain away. He pressed her against him, whispering over and over that she would be all right, that he was there for her. His words gave her a feeling of safety she hadn't experienced in a long time.

When sirens invaded the quiet, Melora managed to pull herself together and step out of his embrace. She swiped the wet tracks from her cheeks and said, "I'll be all right. I need to change and see about Kaitlyn and Juanita."

"I'll take care of the sheriff. We'll find who did this, Melora."

She started up the stairs, her legs wobbly. Clutching the railing, she peered back at Daniel as he made his way toward the front door. What would she have done without him here?

Or was the fact he was here the reason her uncle was dead now?

With Melora, Kaitlyn and Juanita upstairs with Gisella, Daniel stood back with Ranger Levi McDonnell while the body of Tyler Madison was taken from the house. The crime scene was being processed, the pictures taken. He already had someone coming out to replace the window. All the blinds were drawn, and law enforcement officers were out scouring the grounds for any evidence.

"Melora has told me I can do whatever I need to secure this place. Money isn't an object, but she doesn't want to leave until whatever the people are after is found. She wants these people brought to justice." Daniel shut the front door behind the deputies carrying out the body bag.

Levi frowned. "How are we going to keep her safe if we can't hide her somewhere?"

"By protecting her here and finding the flash drive that people are killing to get a hold of. It wasn't on Axle's body when we found him so maybe he's hidden it somewhere. That's what someone thinks and they want it." Daniel paced the entry hall, his nerves pulled taut, as though any second they would snap. "We can have people patrol the grounds and replace some of the windows with bullet-resistant glass. With the other ones we can keep the blinds closed, stay out of those rooms. She's got a good security system, and her doors were already reinforced after the break-in."

"What do you want to do next?"

"They're getting desperate to kill her uncle in her home. Why did they? Another warning? Or was the bullet meant for Melora? No way to tell for sure. I'm going to her uncle's house. She is his heir and has given me permission to do whatever is needed to keep her daughter safe."

"I wish we knew who the killer intended to shoot."

"We need to look into her uncle's affairs. See if

he was the target or Melora." Daniel stopped and faced his fellow Company D Ranger. "She was standing a couple of feet away from her uncle. I need to search his home. See if there's a reason someone would want him dead. I can't rule anything out. I want you and Gisella to stay and guard them. I want two Rangers here at all times until we figure out what's going on. Coordinate the security until I get back and see to any follow-up on searching the grounds. When all the evidence is collected, have Evan hand deliver it to the crime lab in San Antonio."

"Will do."

"I'm going to let Melora know what I'm doing, then leave." Daniel headed toward the stairs and mounted them to the second floor.

With dread he walked toward the den. When he'd left Melora earlier with Gisella, he hated seeing the bleak look in her eyes. She was trying to be upbeat for Kaitlyn, but it was coming out false and the little girl knew it. The child had been unusually quiet.

Stepping just inside the room, he caught Melora's attention while her daughter sat in front of the television watching a movie. Gisella nodded toward him while Melora quickly crossed the room and slipped out into the hall.

"What's going on? Did you all find anything outside?"

Melora's eyes, full of fear, caused his gut to churn. "Not yet but they are still searching. They're through downstairs, however."

"Can Juanita clean up? She doesn't want Kaitlyn to see anything and neither do I."

"That's fine. Ranger McDonnell will be stationed downstairs while I'm gone."

The fright in her gaze took over her whole expression. "Why? Where?"

"I want to check out your uncle's house."

"You think they were after him, not me?" The creases in her forehead deepened.

"Why did he tell you he was sorry? What was he sorry for?"

"I don't know." She kneaded her fingertips into her brow. "Do what you have to. My daughter comes first, and I have to do whatever I can to keep her safe. They may have been threatening Uncle Tyler. He was scared when he talked to me. I've never seen him like that."

He turned to leave. Her hand on his back stopped his movement, and he pivoted toward her.

"Stay safe. I'll call the housekeeper and tell her you're coming."

"Don't." The widening of her eyes caused him to add, "We don't know who to trust."

"Fine. Call me if you need me to say something to her. Remember she's Juanita's older sister."

"What's her name?"

"Carmen Perez."

"Keep Juanita up here with you all. Give me the time to get to your uncle's before telling her she can go downstairs to clean up."

"You can't think she had anything to do with this. My uncle has been wonderful to her and her sister."

"I don't know what to think, Melora." He took her hands in his. "But I do know I'm not taking any chances with your life or Kaitlyn's."

She nodded, some of the fear dimming for a few seconds as she stared into his eyes. "I know. That's why I've put our lives in your hands."

With a quick squeeze, he left her to make his way downstairs and to his truck before he did something foolish like drag her into his arms and never let her go. The vulnerable look in her eyes tore at the wall he'd erected around his heart.

Lord, please keep Melora and Kaitlyn safe.

All he could do right now was turn her protection over to God and try to find some clue that would lead him to the person behind killing Axle and her uncle.

Fifteen minutes later he rang Tyler Madison's doorbell and a slightly older version of Juanita positioned herself in the entrance as though he would have to come through her to get into the mansion.

"Carmen, I'm Ranger Daniel Riley." He showed her his badge. "May I come in to talk?"

"Señor Madison isn't here right now."

"I know. I need to talk to you."

A question darkened her brown eyes. "Me?"

"Yes, ma'am."

Carmen stepped to the side to allow him into the foyer.

Daniel entered and headed for the living room visible off the entryway. The housekeeper followed but hung back by the door. Doubt and suspicion molded her features.

"Why do you want to talk to me?"

Daniel waved his hand toward a chair. "I have some news. You might want to take a seat."

The color leaked from her face. "Has something happened to Melora? Juanita told me you were staying at her house." She took the nearest chair.

He shook his head as he sat across from her. "It's not Melora, but Mr. Madison. He was murdered today at Melora's."

"Señor Madison? Murdered? How?"

"Someone shot him through the window while he was talking to Melora. Do you have an idea why anyone would want to kill Mr. Madison?"

Something unreadable flashed in the woman's eyes, before a composed expression descended over her features. She sat up straight, gripping the arms of the chair. "Señor Madison was a good employer."

"Melora has given me permission to search her uncle's house."

Carmen opened her mouth to say something but instead snapped it closed.

"You can call her if you want to verify that." Daniel delved into his pocket and withdrew his cell.

Carmen rose. "What do you need to see?" Stiff formality marked her bearing.

"First Mr. Madison's office. I understand from Melora he usually worked from home."

The older woman, with hints of gray in her dark hair, pinched her mouth into a frown. "This way. Please don't mess up anything. Señor Madison doesn't like…" Her voice hitched and her lips quivered.

"I'll do my best to leave it as I first saw it."

She opened a dark walnut door and stepped back. "This is," she swallowed hard, "his office."

"Who else is here in the house?"

"No one right now."

"In this huge house?" It was twice the size of Melora's. He knew how many people it took to take care of a home this size because his parents' was as big as Tyler's.

"Señor Madison sent them all away this morning. I just returned home an hour ago. They won't be back until much later."

Interesting. "Do you know why?"

She shook her head. "He took a call in his office then came out and told me to give everyone the day off. He insisted I go visit my daughter, too."

"Please come in and sit while I look through the office."

Her head held high, she gave him a frosty look. "I'm not going to do anything to interfere with your investigation."

"I may have questions for you."

She snorted and settled on to a hardback chair, clasping her hands in her lap.

Daniel felt her gaze on him as he strode to the desk and rummaged through it. Nothing of interest. Glancing at the laptop and seeing it was password protected, he decided to take it with him and give it to one of the Rangers who was a whiz at computers. Next he turned his attention to the filing cabinet behind the desk.

Half an hour later he discovered something that he doubted Melora knew about or she'd kept hidden from him. Her uncle had been a partner in the restaurant chain. What else had Tyler Madison been involved in? The illegal activities taking place through the business? He would have Evan and Oliver dig deeper into Melora's uncle's affairs. There might be a connection to the Lions of Texas. Could that be the reason he'd told her he was sorry? If he were connected to the Lions of Texas, the recent events happening to Melora would have troubled him. He didn't doubt Tyler loved his niece, so did he have a falling-out with someone because he was threatening her?

Daniel continued his search, finishing in the office and moving to the man's bedroom. He wasn't sure how he was going to tell Melora that her uncle might not be an innocent bystander in this whole situation. She was hurting already. This would make it worse.

"Mommy, I wanna show Daniel the stable." Kaitlyn stomped her foot and put her hands on her waist.

"Young lady, that's enough. We can't leave here right now." Melora faced her daughter in the middle of the kitchen, all the blinds shut, relieved most of the people were gone and her house was quiet again.

"Why?"

Because I said so, was on the tip of Melora's tongue, but she gulped back those words and moved toward Kaitlyn. Drawing her toward the table, Melora sat and held her daughter's hands. "Honey, we need to stay here right now. Daniel asked us to."

"Where is he?" Kaitlyn drew her eyebrows

together while her mouth turned down in a pout. "He promised to teach me to play Go Fish." She bent toward Melora and whispered, "Who is that other man here?"

"I told you it was a friend of Daniel's and Gisella's."

"He's big. He wears a star, too."

"Because he's a Texas Ranger like Daniel."

Kaitlyn tilted her head to the right. "What's going on?"

She couldn't keep everything from her daughter, but what should she tell her? The whole truth frightened her, so she could just imagine what Kaitlyn would feel. "Some bad men want something of your daddy's. I don't want them to have it."

"Robbers?" Her daughter's eyes grew round.

"Yeah. But we're safe with Daniel and Gisella. Nothing is going to happen to us." She hoped and prayed.

"I know. Daniel is the good guy."

Yes, he was. A guy who was trying to protect them and get answers to what was going on. But at the same time struggling with his own personal problems. She wished she could help him with Clay. He'd done so much for her and Kaitlyn.

Voices coming from the foyer intruded into Melora's thoughts.

Kaitlyn swiveled her head toward the doorway

into the kitchen. "Daniel's home." She tugged her hands from Melora's and ran out of the room.

Melora heard Daniel's greeting to Kaitlyn and her giggles. What was going to happen when all this was over? Her daughter was really starting to care about Daniel. She'd loved her great uncle Tyler but had never warmed to him as she had with Daniel. She was determined that Kaitlyn wasn't going to get hurt anymore. It was bad enough that the two most important men in her life had been killed. Actually the same could be said for herself. Melora rose, resolved to keep her emotional distance and help Kaitlyn do the same. Somehow.

Daniel's large frame filled the kitchen entrance. Kaitlyn stood slightly in front of him with his hand on her shoulder. A huge grin transformed her daughter's earlier expression into one of excitement and happiness. How was she going to tell Kaitlyn that Uncle Tyler was dead?

"Daniel's gonna teach me Go Fish."

The sight of her daughter's eyes sparkling as though everything was right with the world brought home how important it was to keep as much as possible from her. *Lord, give me the wisdom to say the right thing.*

Gisella appeared behind Daniel. "I thought you were going to show me your stuffed animals."

"Oh, yeah." Kaitlyn leaned back and looked up at Daniel. "Can we play Go Fish after dinner?"

"Sounds like a plan to me."

Kaitlyn went to Gisella, and they started for the stairs.

"Are you staying here now, too?" her daughter asked the Texas Ranger.

"Yeah. Is that okay?" Gisella asked.

"Some of my friends have had sleepovers. Kinda like that?"

"Yes." But the rest of what Gisella said faded as the pair went up to the second floor.

Daniel's gaze zeroed in on Melora. "Are you all right?"

"Yes," she automatically said, then realized how false that was. She sank down into the chair and shook her head. "No, I'm not."

He sat next to her and scooted closer so they faced each other. Linking their hands together he said, "What have you told Kaitlyn? I don't want to say anything you don't want her to know."

"Nothing about today other than some bad men are after something of her daddy's. I haven't told her about Uncle Tyler. I don't know how to—not on top of what happened to Axle. Although he was her father, she hadn't seen him in two years and had already gone through some grieving before it was official he was dead. That's not the case with my uncle. Any suggestions?"

His thumbs ran across the back of her hands.

"I'm the last person to ask advice where it concerns a child. You know how things are with Clay."

"When this is over with, you and Clay should come to dinner. Kaitlyn would think it's a treat. One of her friends has an older brother and she has mentioned on more than one occasion that she wants a brother or sister."

"I can remember when Clay was a young boy right before his mother and I separated, how much he wanted a little brother to play with. He didn't like being an only child." One corner of his mouth tilted upward. "I hated being an only child, too. It can get mighty lonely."

"So are you beating yourself up over the fact you didn't give your son a sibling to play with?"

Daniel blinked. "According to him that was one of the many things I didn't give him. The top of his list was my attention. The problem with that is he was right. As my marriage fell apart, I spent more and more time at work. I wanted to become a Texas Ranger, and I knew there were only so many selected and that my father would try to stop me from doing that. He kept hoping I would give up my dream of working in law enforcement and join him in his company. Another person I couldn't please." Combing his fingers through his hair, he grimaced. "It seems to me I have a habit of leaving unfinished business between me and the people I care about. My dad died before we ever settled our differences."

"And you don't want something like that to happen with you and Clay?"

"Something like that. I regret my father and I didn't reconcile and I don't want my son to ever feel that way. There's no way to change it now."

"Please do think about coming to dinner when things are settled."

"What are you up to?" Daniel asked with a grin.

"You've done so much for me. I thought I would return the favor."

"And be a referee between Clay and me?"

"No, just facilitate you two getting to know each other better. It'll give my daughter something to look forward to. She misses her friends, especially Cara. I wish I could have Jorge, Beth and Cara over for dinner, but we'll just have to wait until this is all over with. I can't deal with others right now and play the gracious hostess like nothing is wrong. I know Jorge and Beth would understand but…" She couldn't finish her sentence, knowing in her heart no one should come to her house—not after what happened to Uncle Tyler. All that had transpired recently overwhelmed her.

He tightened his grasp on her hands. "I know this is hard on you and what I have to tell you isn't going to make this any easier."

TEN

Daniel looked away, his jaw set in a hard line. "You aren't going to like it." He drew in a deep breath. "Your uncle was a partner in the restaurant chain. Did you know that?"

The accusation in his voice sliced through the haze his announcement had first created in her. She yanked her hands from his and bolted to her feet. "No. Are you sure about that? My uncle would have told me an important detail like..." She remembered all the times he tried to convince her not to sell, to keep things as they were. Why would he keep that a secret from her? She would have sold him the whole business. Shaking her head, she collapsed back into the chair. "I don't understand all this. I can see Axle keeping stuff from me. He never wanted me to be involved in his affairs. Went out of his way to keep his business and family life separate." She flipped her hand in the air. "Of course, now I see why."

"I hate to say this, but your uncle might have

been involved in the illegal side of your husband's business as well. Maybe he was trying to protect you from it."

"We don't even know what the illegal business is for sure. We haven't found anything definite."

Daniel dropped his gaze to his lap. "Not exactly. The Ranger who has been going through the books we got from the business found one of your husband's suppliers has drug cartel connections. It isn't obvious but after some digging we uncovered a company that ties the supplier to a lieutenant in a drug cartel in northern Mexico."

"What are you saying? He was smuggling in drugs through food shipments?" The series of shocks inundating her made her want to curl up in a ball and hide.

"He's running down some things and should have something for me in a couple of days. But yes, I think that might be it. We've had other indications that drugs are tied up in all of this. What we need to know now is where the drugs come from and where they go."

She squeezed her hands so tightly that her fingernails dug into her palms. "I could believe that of Axle but my uncle…" Inhaling deeply, she fortified herself for what she had to face. "Is that why Uncle Tyler told me he was sorry? That he put me and Kaitlyn in danger with his illegal activities?"

"That's a good possibility. Why else did he plead

with you to stop working with us? To let him protect you? Maybe he's been protecting you these past two years, and he couldn't any longer. It's obvious someone is going to great lengths to find Axle's flash drive before we do."

The pounding against her skull increased to a maddening tempo as though proclaiming her doom. She couldn't deal with all of this now. Again, she came to her feet although her legs barely held her up. "I'd better check on Kaitlyn. I don't want her to talk Gisella's ear off."

"I asked Gisella to keep her occupied while I talked to you. Kaitlyn is all right. But I'm not so sure about you."

The softly spoken statement, full of concern, wrecked what composure she had. She barely felt Daniel take her hands in his and guide her to sit. What a sheltered life she had led! Axle and her uncle must have had a good laugh about how naive she was. "Maybe Uncle Tyler didn't know what was going on? Maybe he began to suspect lately and…" A hysterical laugh escaped her throat. "Who am I kidding? My uncle would know about what was going on with any of his investments. He's sharp. What am I going to do?"

"Nothing right now. When we get hard evidence, we'll make a move. But to tell you the truth, I have a feeling that William Thompson shut down any drug operations once we carted off all the paperwork."

"So you think William is part of it, too?"

"Maybe. I have to assume that until proven otherwise. Your uncle hired him to run the restaurant chain. It could all be connected."

"I need to make arrangements to bury Uncle Tyler. I have to do something. He had it all set up so I don't have to plan it, but I need to go. Is that possible?"

"I would like to say no, but I'd rather keep whoever is behind this guessing at what we know and are doing. I think we can manage protecting you. We do have some experience in that area with protecting the governor."

"Who will likely come to the funeral."

Daniel frowned. "Along with a lot of other important people. Maybe the very people behind all of this. Did you ever hear Axle talk about the Lions of Texas?"

Melora closed her eyes and thought back to the time Quin had come into the house when Axle and he had argued. A faint memory teased her—just out of her reach. "Maybe."

"When? What did you hear?"

She kneaded her temples, the hammering of her headache intensifying until she couldn't think straight. "I think Quin mentioned them when he talked to Axle right before he went missing." Her eyes popped open. "But I can't be sure. It sounds familiar, but I don't remember exactly why."

He replaced her hands with his and massaged slow circles on her forehead. "Don't force it. It'll come to you sooner or later." His fingers combed through her hair and gently cradled her. "Right now you need to see to burying your uncle. I ask one thing. Please keep Kaitlyn here with Gisella."

Her gaze glued to his, she nodded. His touch robbed her of any coherent thoughts. All she wanted to do was surrender to him, give her heart to him. She couldn't, not with what was going on, but that didn't squelch the need to be cherished that burned inside her. "I agree. She has gone through enough with Axle's funeral. I'll have to say something tonight, though, to her about Uncle Tyler. I just don't know what."

He settled his hands on her shoulders. "You'll come up with the right thing to say. You and your daughter have a good relationship."

"And so can you with your son. Remember, we'll have dinner after the person who has been after me is caught."

His eyes softened. "Thank you for caring. I don't think it will help, but I appreciate the thought anyway."

"Daniel Boone Riley, do I hear you giving up?"

His mouth fell open, his eyes round. "Never. That isn't in my nature."

"Good, because one day what you say to Clay will work. Just don't give up on having a relationship with him. You are not your father."

"And one day this will be over, and you'll get on with your life. Safe. Free."

His words were music to her ears. She wanted that so much. Didn't quite understand why the Lord would put her—and especially Kaitlyn—through this nightmare in the first place. Her daughter was an innocent in all of this and could be hurt. *I'm the one who married Axle. I'm the one who ignored the warning signs. Not Kaitlyn, Lord. Please keep her safe at least.*

The sounds of Kaitlyn and Gisella coming back into the kitchen turned Melora away from Daniel to face the doorway. She plastered a smile on her face, determined to keep everything as normal as possible.

"She's got quite a collection of stuffed animals. Enough for her own zoo," Gisella said as they entered.

"Shh. Don't say that too loud, or she'll be wanting you to play zoo with her tonight." Melora opened her arms for Kaitlyn.

"Yes! We need to." Her daughter hugged her, beaming. "After dinner."

"Speaking of dinner, Juanita wanted to be awakened in time to prepare it. Honey, can you go get her?"

"What are we having?" Kaitlyn stepped back.

"Spaghetti and meatball casserole is what she told me earlier."

Her daughter ran from the room. She could hear her footfalls on the tiled floor as she hurried down the hall to Juanita's room, then the sounds of her knocking on the door.

At that moment, Ranger Levi McDonnell came into the kitchen from the other part of the house. "I'll be heading out now that you're here. There will be two men outside."

"I'll meet with you tomorrow about security at the funeral," Daniel said.

"Mommy!" Kaitlyn yelled from the back hallway.

Melora jerked around and started toward the hallway off the kitchen when Kaitlyn rushed back into the room. Melora's heartbeat accelerated.

"Juanita isn't in her room."

"What?" Melora passed her daughter to go back to the housekeeper's suite.

"She left earlier to go to the store to pick up some items for dinner tonight."

Levi's words stopped Melora in her tracks. She swiveled around. "What items? She already has it made and only has to put it in the oven and make a salad."

"She didn't say. I let her go since she isn't…" The

Ranger glanced at Kaitlyn and paused, inhaling a breath.

Gisella approached Kaitlyn. "Let's leave them to figure out dinner." Taking the little girl's hand, she led her toward the doorway. "We could set up the zoo, so we can play after dinner."

"What about Juanita?" Kaitlyn asked.

After the pair was out of earshot, Melora faced both Daniel and Levi. "Yeah, what about Juanita? There wasn't any reason for her to leave. What if she is in danger? She's like a member of my family." Her fear spiked at the thought of something happening to Juanita, too. "Do you think she is scared and has run?"

"Does she carry a cell?" Daniel headed down the hallway to Juanita's room.

"Yes." Melora stepped into her housekeeper's living quarters and realized she rarely came into the suite.

Daniel made a beeline for the dresser where a note and a cell sat. Lifting up the note by the corner, he read, "I can't stay, Melora. Too much has happened. Don't try to find me. I'll be fine. Keep safe, Juanita." He swung around and looked at Melora then Levi. "She must realize a cell has a GPS that can track her."

"And she doesn't want to be tracked? Why does she think she's in danger?" Levi crossed the bedroom and checked her calls on the phone. "The last person she talked with was Carmen Perez."

"That's her sister. The one who works for Tyler Madison. She received a call as I was finishing up going through Tyler's house. It must have been Juanita."

"I'll take Oliver and go question the sister. We'll do another look around the house, too."

"You think Juanita went to Uncle Tyler's?" Heartache gripped her and wouldn't let go. With each bit of news Melora got, it pounded even more as though someone was knocking urgently on a door.

Levi shook his head. "No, probably not."

"But your uncle's house is a big one. I couldn't cover the whole place. I focused on his office, bedroom and den where Carmen said he spent most of his time."

"Also out in the greenhouse. He raised orchids and was out there every day he was in town." Melora backed up until she sat on her housekeeper's bed, untouched as if she'd never had any intention of resting when she came to her room. All the people around her weren't who she had thought they were. Everything was a lie. Where would this trail of lies lead to? Death or salvation?

"Did he have a safe or any place he kept important papers besides his office?" Daniel asked as Levi took the cell and note then left the room.

"No safe that I knew of, but he did have a safety deposit box at his bank."

"We can get a court order to open the box. Maybe there's something in it. Did you ever check and see if Axle had one other than the one you and your uncle opened?"

"No. I never found evidence of another one. As I told you earlier, the one Axle and I shared didn't have anything relevant to this in it. The deed to the house—some other papers like that. I figured if there was anything, it was here. Like Uncle Tyler, Axle rarely worked from his office at his company headquarters."

"I'll have someone run that down. There might be a safety deposit box in another bank you don't know about."

"With Axle anything is possible. He was a very private man." As was her uncle. Melora clutched the edge of the bed, her fingernails digging into the soft coverlet. How could she trust any feelings for Daniel that were developing when she'd been so totally wrong about others?

Kaitlyn ran into the room with Gisella a few steps behind her. "Mommy, did you find Juanita?"

"She's gone to visit a friend for a while. You, young lady, can help me make a salad for dinner." Melora shoved herself off the bed and grasped her daughter's hand. "I don't know about you but I'm starving." As Melora left, she threw a look back at

Daniel and Gisella, their heads bent toward each other. They talked quietly.

In that moment, Melora realized if it hadn't been for Daniel's persistence with her, she and possibly Kaitlyn would be dead by now. A cold wave flooded her, and she quaked.

Later that night, Melora tucked Kaitlyn into the bed. "We're going to put up the Christmas tree in a few days and guess who said he would come help us?"

"Who?" Kaitlyn yawned.

"Daniel."

Kaitlyn clapped, suddenly wide awake. "Yippee. Can we go see the Nutcracker this year? Cara's going with her mom."

"I don't know, honey. We need to stay close to home for the time being."

"Why, Mommy?"

"Lots of things are happening. Uncle Tyler went home to Jesus today."

"Like Daddy?"

Melora nodded.

Kaitlyn frowned. "When? He was here earlier and left without saying goodbye. Was that why all those people were here today?"

"Yes. It was sudden or he would have said goodbye to you. He loved you very much. We need to say a prayer for him."

"And Daddy." Kaitlyn folded her hands together. "God, tell Daddy and Uncle Tyler I love them. Amen." She peered at Melora. "When will I get to see them again?"

Tears closed her throat. She didn't know what to say to Kaitlyn. When Axle had died, she'd had a long talk about people dying and going to live with God. That one day Kaitlyn would see her loved ones again.

"Only God knows when, honey."

"I'm gonna draw Uncle Tyler and Daddy, too, a picture. I can give it to them when I see them again."

"I'm sure they would love it, but it may be a long time."

Stifling another yawn, her daughter snuggled under the covers. "That's okay. I'm pat…" She screwed her mouth into a thoughtful expression. "I can wait."

Melora kissed her. "Yes, you are patient."

After switching off the lamp, in the soft glow from the night-light she made her way to the door. Throwing a glance back at Kaitlyn, she saw her daughter clutch Mr. Snuggles and close her eyes.

When she returned to the kitchen where she'd left Daniel and Gisella, she only found Daniel. "Where's Gisella?"

"I sent her home to pack some belongings since she'll be staying here, too. She'll be back later.

She's allergic to cats, so she's got to pick up some meds."

Melora walked to the stove and poured some hot water then retrieved an herbal tea bag from a cabinet to make a soothing drink before going to bed. "I got hold of the funeral home and we'll have the service at Lone Star Christian Church. Uncle Tyler occasionally attended with Kaitlyn and me. It's big enough for a large crowd."

"When?"

"Saturday." She sank into a chair next to Daniel at the table. "The last thing I want to do is go to another funeral. Uncle Tyler didn't want a big fuss. I'll respect his wishes and keep it as simple as possible."

Daniel toyed with the handle on his mug. "I got a call from Levi right before dinner. I didn't want to say anything until he knew more, and I didn't want Kaitlyn to overhear us talking."

Melora clasped her drink and brought it to her lips. The heat from the cup barely warming her cold fingers. "I'm not going to like this, am I?"

He shook his head. "When they arrived, Carmen wasn't there. They thought she would return before they left, but she didn't."

"Did they get to go inside?"

"That's what was strange. The front door was unlocked."

"And you think something has happened to Carmen?"

"Maybe."

Her hands trembled as she placed her mug on the table. "Was there any evidence of foul play?"

"No, and Carmen's clothes aren't in her closet and drawers."

"Is it the same as with Alicia? Where someone made it appear as though she left in a hurry?"

"In this case I think Carmen really did. I think she met up with Juanita."

"She had a blue Chevy she kept in the garage. Is it still there?"

"Yeah, but the security tape showed a cab picking up Carmen not twenty minutes after I left. Levi is checking with the cab company to see where the driver took Carmen."

She scrubbed her hands down her face, numb from the onslaught of emotions that had bombarded her the past few weeks. "So the question is why did Carmen and Juanita run?"

"And where to? We need to find them. They could be in danger."

"Or they know something about what's really going on. Maybe they're as involved as it appears Uncle Tyler was." Defeat and sorrow sagged her shoulders.

"Which only reinforces my feeling they're in danger. People connected to this case are dying."

For a while through dinner her headache had subsided. Now it returned full force, beating a loud tempo against her skull. Even the soothing effect of the herbal tea could do nothing to calm her tattered nerves.

"Do you have any idea where Juanita would go if she was in trouble?"

"A lot of her family is still in Mexico."

"So you think she might have gone there?"

"Maybe. She loved living here and was so proud when she became a citizen, but if she feared for her life, she might go back."

"While you were putting Kaitlyn down for bed, I put out an alert to the border patrol about Juanita and Carmen Perez. If they try to cross legally, I'll know where."

"But there are a lot of miles of border between the U.S. and Mexico, and if they didn't want anyone to know they left here, they could try crossing illegally." Her mind felt crowded with fear, weariness and betrayal, each vying for supremacy. Suddenly, she didn't know what she should do, as if every time she came to a decision something else happened to make the situation worse. The temptation to shut totally down inundated her. "So what do we do now?" Even to her own ears she heard the exhaustion in every word she uttered.

Daniel rose and, taking her hands, pulled her to her feet. "Right now you need to get some rest. Tomorrow will be a busy day with funeral arrangements, people wanting to offer their condolences."

"But we need to find what Axle left behind."

"I'll continue to look. You don't need to worry about anything. Take care of your family."

She gripped him, the tactile connection comforting as if she wasn't totally alone in the world. "Finding that is taking care of my family. Kaitlyn and I aren't safe as long as it is still out there and people are looking for it."

"I understand your need, and you can help when you're able to."

"We've already looked through half this house and nothing. What if we don't find anything here? What if the person who killed Axle took the flash drive?"

"I think this is all connected to the Lions of Texas and the person who killed Axle is part of that group." He drew her toward the doorway. "We haven't looked everywhere yet. You're worrying about something that hasn't happened. I've found worrying is wasted energy."

"So what do you suggest I do?" she asked, placing her foot on the bottom stair.

"Pray. Let the Lord take your worries. He's much more capable than us to deal with them."

"That's supposed to take my worries away?"

In the middle of the staircase, Daniel faced her

and clasped her upper arms. "Yes. Do you have a better idea?"

"How do I do that?"

"Talk to God. Tell Him your problems then give them to Him. Let Him work on them for you."

"Have you done that?"

"I'm working on it with my situation with Clay."

"But you haven't totally."

He stared over her shoulder, a thoughtful expression in his eyes. "You know a week ago I would have told you no, but more and more I have been. I think you've helped that."

"How?"

"You seem determined to see me and Clay mend our relationship. Your suggestions on how are good ones."

A grin that made his eyes sparkle blanketed her in warmth. "I've always been a worrier. It won't be easy to do."

"What harm will happen if you try? It might help." He resumed his ascent up the stairs.

At the second-floor landing Daniel led her toward her room. "I'm staying up until Gisella gets back. You're safe. There are two guards outside, and I'll make sure the house is secured. Get some sleep." He stopped at her door and faced her. "Don't worry. We'll figure this out. There are a lot of Rangers in Company D who want to make sure this works out."

She peered up at him and the need to be held overpowered her common sense. "Will you hold me?" The words came out before she could stop them.

Without hesitation he drew her into his embrace and pressed her close to him. "That, ma'am, I can accommodate," he said in his Texan drawl.

She listened to the beating of his heart and it soothed her, as though it flowed from him to her—steady, strong. She could get used to this. She could so easily fall in love with Daniel.

That thought brought back the common sense that had fled. Look what had happened the last time she thought she was in love. She stepped away, gave him a shaky smile and quickly went into her bedroom. Leaning against the door, she closed her eyes and could smell his aftershave, a light lime scent that enveloped her in that warmth she drew from him.

Oh, she was in more trouble than she realized. She was falling in love as her life was falling apart around her.

ELEVEN

"What are you going to do with all these boxes?" Daniel asked the morning of the funeral as he swept his hand over the stacked cartons in Melora's garage.

Melora, with her hands on her waist, scanned all the containers with Axle's possessions from the house. "The ones with a red star I'll keep for Kaitlyn. When she gets older, she can decide how much she wants to keep of her father's. The rest are going to the homeless shelter. I hope others can benefit from Axle's clothes. Something good has to come out of all this." She pivoted toward him. "But we've been through the whole house and found nothing."

Rubbing the back of his neck, Daniel frowned. "Yeah and our search for another safety deposit box didn't turn up anything. Nor have we found Juanita and Carmen, Alicia Wells or Gordon Johnson."

"What if the bodyguard killed Axle then left

the country? He could have been paid or maybe he and Axle had some kind of falling-out. Axle could be very demanding."

"Or he could be dead and his body hasn't been found yet. We've expanded the search outward from where Axle was found."

A sigh escaped her lips. "At least we now know that Uncle Tyler and my husband were business partners, that my uncle helped finance the chain eight years ago. And neither one ever said a word to me. Which makes me think my uncle was involved with whatever my husband was caught up in."

"Are you ready for this afternoon?"

"Yes, I still owe Uncle Tyler for taking me in when my parents died, but I feel used. He's the one who introduced me to Axle and encouraged me to date him. Sometimes I wonder if I married Axle for my uncle's approval. And then I begin to wonder if it came down to me or Axle, who would my uncle have chosen?" That thought had kept her up a good part of the night before. She'd spent another sleepless night pacing her bedroom, staring up at the dark ceiling with images of the past flittering in and out of her mind.

"If Tyler hadn't cared for you, he wouldn't have come that day to your house to try and get you to back off. I think that was his way of trying to protect you from what was happening."

"Are you just saying that to make me feel

better? It could have been his way of protecting himself."

"Maybe. But in the end he was asking for your forgiveness. That doesn't sound like a man totally looking out for himself."

Her shoulders sagged with the weight she felt pressing down on her. "I'm firing William Thompson. It's clear he knows something about what's going on."

"We're keeping tabs on him and checking into his background and finances. We don't have enough to charge him yet, though."

Melora headed for the door into the house. "With nothing turning up in the house, where do we go from here?"

"The cabana, stable and any place you can think of that meant something to your husband. But not until tomorrow."

"Yeah, I have to get through the funeral that's in," she checked her watch, "two hours." In the kitchen she paused at the island, gripping its edge. "Have you ever felt torn by duty and what you really wanted to do?"

His laugh came out humorless. "Countless times, especially when it came to my son and father."

"I hate being away from Kaitlyn. I like her nearby."

His eyes gleaming with sympathy, he approached

her, invading her personal space. "She'll be safe here with Gisella and the guards outside."

"I'm glad the governor had business in Washington. I assured him I didn't want him to cancel those plans."

"And I, along with all the other Texas Rangers, appreciate that." Daniel clasped her arms. "I will make sure you're safe. I'm not letting anything happen to you today. We'll pull right up to the doors. There is only a short distance to the building."

"What if it's someone attending the funeral?"

"Unless he doesn't care about getting away, it wouldn't be the place to try anything." He ran his hand down her arm and captured hers, twining his fingers through hers. "I'll be right next to you the whole time."

His words wrapped about her as though he embraced her. This man before her was strong, protective, caring. She could get so used to that in her life, but when this was over with, reality would return. Right now everything seemed surreal and she shouldn't trust her growing feelings for him. "Thank you for every—"

Kaitlyn came into the kitchen with Gisella right behind her. "Gisella and me set up the zoo again. Can you and Daniel come to it?"

"Sure. I have some time before I have to leave."

Playing with her daughter would be a perfect way to take her mind off the funeral.

Kaitlyn hurried out of the room and Melora started for the doorway when Daniel's cell sounded. She stopped and glanced back while he answered the call. A frown carved itself deep into his face as he listened to the person on the other end.

When he hung up, he peered at her. "Alicia's body has been found."

"Where?"

"A couple of miles from her apartment in a wooded area. Someone dug a shallow grave for her that some dogs unearthed. Two teenagers found the body and reported it to the police. She was shot."

"Which confirms she must have given the man my code and her key."

"Yep, it appears that way."

Another person she knew was dead. "When will this end?" Numb, she murmured a question to which there was no answer.

Sitting in the front pew with Daniel next to her, Melora listened to "Amazing Grace," the last song for the funeral service before people began to file past the coffin and pay their respects to her uncle. As the final note sounded, the emotions she'd held in check for the past hour swelled in her like the ending of the song. Why had she chosen "Amazing

Grace"? It always made her cry, but she remembered that it was her uncle's favorite hymn. She owed him even if he'd lied to her.

The first group of people viewed her uncle.

"Okay?" Daniel whispered in her ear.

Okay? No. The numbness she'd felt when she'd heard about Alicia had spread, taking over every inch of her. "I'll be better when I get home."

The words to the song had made her cry, not the death of her uncle. She couldn't seem to wrap her mind around the fact he was gone, too. It was surreal, as though this was all happening to someone else. She dabbed at her eyes and sat up straighter, preparing herself to greet everyone. She wasn't going to let this get the best of her.

Before she could answer Daniel, Hank Zarvy and his wife stopped in front of her. Hank cupped her hand between his. "Melora, I'm so sorry about Tyler. He was a friend. I'll miss him."

"Thank you. I appreciate you all coming today." The mechanical tone to her voice only reinforced her sense of going through the motions on autopilot. Even when Jorge and Beth followed Hank and his wife and offered their condolences, she couldn't dismiss the feeling someone else was shaking hands and accepting people's sympathy.

For the next few minutes somehow Melora said what was expected, shook hands and didn't fall apart in front of the mourners. Then Rodney

Tanner paused in front of her. He had been a close friend of her uncle's.

Fury marked his expression as he greeted her. "I still can't believe it. I'd just talked to him a few hours before it happened. I…" The man swallowed hard, his eyes misting. "Some of us have thought of offering a reward for—"

The fire alarm blasted through the church, a red light flashing. Someone shouted in the back, "I smell smoke." It sounded as if that person had smoked a pack of cigarettes.

The words jolted her with a memory—vague, just out of her reach, but she was too tired to think straight.

Panic descended on Rodney's face while he scanned the area. People near him began pushing him as they made their way toward the aisle. He swept along on the wave of mourners trying to get out of the one set of double doors into the sanctuary.

Daniel grabbed Melora's hand. "Stay close."

Tugging her to her feet, he dived into the mob surging for the exit with her plastered against his side. The next thing she realized Levi was next to her. All numbness fled to be replaced with a heart-thudding fear.

Someone bumped into her. Melora stumbled. Daniel's arm went around her and held her up.

As she neared the doors that led out into the foyer, the scent of smoke grew stronger.

A large man behind her shoved at her. "Move faster. There's a fire."

The people around the man caught the word fire and began pushing the ones in front of them.

"Have the car brought around the side exit," Daniel said to Levi while he kept his arm around Melora, protecting her from the jostling.

Finally out in the church foyer, Daniel gripped her arm and directed her toward the hallway that led to the classrooms and the side exit. A few others were running down the corridor toward that door while most of the crowd poured out of the main entrance.

"Is the car there?" Daniel peered back at Levi taking up the rear.

"Yes."

As they cleared the mass of people in the foyer, Daniel picked up speed down the hall. The exit loomed before them. Three couples left by the same way, a momentary stream of sunshine flooding the dim corridor before the door shut again. When two women went out, Melora saw the front bumper of the black SUV she'd come to the funeral in parked close to the building.

At the door, hand on the knob, Daniel peered at her. "Once I check out the area, I don't want any hesitation. Get to the car and get inside."

She nodded, her pulse thundering so loudly she was surprised she heard him. She knew getting in and out of the armored vehicle was the most dangerous part of the trip.

Daniel let his hand slip off the handle. Something didn't feel right. His nape pricked with a warning. Swiveling around, the arm he held around Melora dropping to his side, Daniel locked gazes with a medium-sized, skinny man, dressed in black slacks, white shirt and long dark coat that fell to his boots. A black cowboy hat sat low on his forehead, shadowing his face. The newcomer slowed his step.

Recognition dawned in Daniel. He was the young man who had been watching Melora. In the next instant, he pushed Melora toward the last classroom in the hallway, yelled at Levi to protect her and went for his gun at the same time the man in black drew out a short-barrel shotgun.

Moving now, Daniel aimed at the intruder and got off a shot as he dove into the classroom behind Levi and Melora. A spray of buckshot peppered the door frame. Crouching by the entrance into the room, Daniel listened to Levi call for backup and the running footsteps of the man in the corridor. Growing closer. He took a deep breath and peeked out, his gun leveled.

Another blast from the shotgun splintered the wood near Daniel's right ear. Lining up the man in his sights, he pulled the trigger. The bullet striking his leg only slowed the man down a couple of steps. He kept coming.

Now he could see the man's eyes—red, wild-looking as though he were on something. He pumped his shotgun again and this time Daniel went flat on the floor as the pellets spewed into the room.

"Get her back," Daniel shouted.

No time to make sure Melora was as safe as possible in the room, Daniel rose slightly and swung out to shoot again. He shot him in the chest this time. Finally, the man stopped, staggered back a few paces then came forward, raising his weapon.

Daniel steadied himself and squeezed off another round. A bright red spot growing on his white shirt, the assailant halted, upright for a few seconds before he collapsed to the tiled floor. Daniel rushed to the shooter and kicked his shotgun away from him, then bent down to feel for his pulse.

The man grabbed Daniel's hand, gripping it for several heartbeats before all strength flowed from his grasp and the life left his body. He stared at the ceiling.

Rangers from both ends of the hallway poured into the corridor. Daniel took a deep breath and stood.

"Daniel." Melora flung herself at him, her arms going around him. "Are you hurt?"

"No."

"You're bleeding."

"I am?" Then he felt the sting from the splintered wood in his cheek and reached up to touch it. Blood coated his fingertips. "It's nothing."

Levi thrust a tissue into his hand. "Get her out of here. I'll clean up this, and let you know who this dude is and how he got in here with a gun."

Daniel pressed the tissue to his cheek while he wound his arm around Melora and headed for the door. After carefully scanning the area, he hurried her to the waiting SUV, the driver, a Texas Ranger, still in it.

"Let's get out of here." Daniel slid in next to Melora in the backseat.

The driver gunned the engine and sped away from the church.

"Let me see your wound." Melora's soft lilting voice washed through him as though it were the only balm to heal him.

She opened her purse and removed a moist cloth from its package and patted at his wound.

"What else are you carrying in there? The rest of a first aid kit?" he asked to lighten the mood. After what just occurred, he desperately needed that.

"Well, let's see. Bandages, antiseptic and a few

other necessary items if you have an active five-year-old with you."

He chuckled. "I hope you aren't referring to me."

The sides of her full lips turned down. "I'm glad you can laugh after what just happened."

He sobered, the scene from the church hallway flooding his thoughts. In all his years as a law enforcement officer, he'd never had to shoot some-one. He'd only wanted to stop him, but the man had kept on coming. The thought of the shooter getting close to Melora still chilled him. "There was nothing funny about that. He could have killed you."

She looked him in the eye. "He could have killed *you*."

Silence, for a long moment, charged the air between them. His focus was totally centered on her beautiful face, full of concern.

"I know one thing—it was either him or us. He wasn't leaving without taking us out." *Taking you out.*

"What he did was bold. He had to realize he could get hurt with all that security in place."

The memory of the man's crazed look filled his mind. "I don't think he was thinking straight. I'm sure he was on drugs, especially by the way he kept coming toward me even after I shot him twice. Probably PCP."

"I think he was the man watching me. Maybe the one who broke into my house."

"His build fits. He looks similar to the sketch you gave of him."

"What color were his eyes?"

"Brown."

Melora dug in her purse, withdrew a tube and squirted some of its contents on the tip of her index finger. "The same as the man who attacked me." She smoothed the antiseptic cream over his cut.

Daniel blew out a frustrated breath. "I wanted to capture him alive. Maybe he would have told us who hired him."

"So you think that man was only following orders?"

"Yeah."

Her gaze fastened on to his. "How do you do this day in, day out?"

"For people like you. I always wanted to be a Texas Ranger. My father used to regale me with stories of Texan history, and I became fascinated by the Texas Rangers as a boy." The day he told his father he was going to follow his dream still was imprinted firmly in his mind. "He loved Texas, but he didn't want me to become a highway patrolman and he made that very clear to me. He threatened to use his power to keep me out. That's when I made it clear I would find a way around him."

"With my uncle I did everything he wanted—even

marrying Axle. I now realize I saw Axle through rose-colored glasses. Because Uncle Tyler wanted us together, I did, too. What a mistake." She twisted her hands together in her lap.

All he wanted to do was draw her into his arms and comfort her. Make her forget the past few years—scared, trapped in a life she couldn't get out of. "My mistake was becoming my father when dealing with Clay. I thought all I needed to do was tell my son what he should do, that was what a father's job was. And look at the mess I made of everything." Which only confirmed he had no business being a father. His job was his life and he needed to be satisfied with that. As much as he wanted to hold her, the realization stressed how important it was to keep his emotional distance from Melora.

"At least my marriage produced one good thing, Kaitlyn. She's been worth all the hurt. I would do anything for her."

Daniel sat forward scouring the area, not far from the entrance into the Lone Star Estates. "Clay and I might not be getting along, but I know what you mean. The day he was born changed me forever. I was suddenly responsible for another human being. It alters your perspective."

"Having Kaitlyn has made me realize how much I want to be a mother. I don't want her to be an only child like I was."

Melora wanted more children. He shouldn't be surprised by that. She was a good mother.

The gates to the estates loomed before the SUV. The driver pulled up and punched in the security code that Melora had given him.

"A statement will have to be issued about the disruption at the funeral. Your uncle was well known in San Antonio." Daniel leaned back, laying his head on the seat cushion. As his surge of adrenaline subsided, a throbbing behind his eyes pulsated to a rapid tempo.

"I'm glad to be back here," Melora said with a sigh. "There's so much that still needs to be done."

He was glad to be back at Melora's, too. A sense of coming home enveloped him for a few seconds—until alarm overcame it. This wasn't his home—could never be. Melora needed a life of calm—a man who could be a good husband to her and a father to Kaitlyn and the children she wanted to have.

"You have worn my daughter out," Melora said the next afternoon as she reentered the living room where Daniel and Gisella were meeting with Levi about the developments in the case since the funeral. Thankfully, her church hadn't been burned down because of what happened. The fire had been confined to two large trashcans in the rec hall.

"She rarely takes a nap, but the second she laid her head on the pillow she was sound asleep."

"Then you can join us." Standing at the French door that led to the deck, Daniel turned from it and smiled, weariness about his eyes.

Melora wished she could erase the tired lines from his face, but he'd been up a good part of the night, coordinating the efforts to locate the gunman's residence after he'd been identified yesterday. She sat on the sofa, and Daniel joined her. Having him close gave her the sense of safety she needed to function. She still felt she had a target plastered on her back.

"Levi just told us that Clyde Walker used to work at your restaurant on the Riverwalk." Daniel relaxed back against the couch.

Having a name for the man who had terrorized her gave her a sense this was almost over with. That she and Kaitlyn might get their lives back soon. "How long ago did he work at the restaurant?" Another connection to Axle's business.

"Six months ago. He told the manager when he quit he had a better job offer."

"Doing what?"

"Working for William Thompson from what a friend said. We're checking on that and hope there's a paper trail we can follow."

The manager her uncle hired to run the business. Although after all that had happened, she shouldn't be surprised, but she was. How many times would she feel betrayed by people who should have loved her and wanted her safe? First Axle and now Uncle Tyler. Who could she believe anymore?

"How did the guy get into the church with a shotgun?" Melora asked, knowing the careful security details the Texas Rangers had gone through before the funeral as they checked the church and each attendant. Although the governor hadn't attended the funeral, he'd made it clear the safety of the people there was a primary concern for the Texas Rangers.

Levi frowned. "A side door had been unlocked. The Ranger who was guarding it was knocked out. Someone in the church most likely took care of Trevor and let Walker inside."

"Is the Ranger okay?" Melora asked, hating the fact another person had been harmed.

"More upset someone got the drop on him than anything else. That and the fact that the doctor kept him overnight in the hospital." Levi clasped the arm of his chair. "We'll find who did this."

"We can place Clyde Walker's car near Alicia's apartment the day she disappeared." Daniel leaned forward. "Some of the traffic cams show his car near there. A neighbor saw her in the morning, and we found her place cleared out in the afternoon. He was in the vicinity right after noon, which means he could have done it. Better yet, he got gas not far from where the body was discovered later that same day. Forensics is checking his vehicle for any blood or trace evidence connecting him directly to Alicia."

"What about Uncle Tyler? Do you have an idea where he was the day my uncle was murdered?"

"There was a rifle in the trunk of his car that matches the caliber of one used to kill your uncle. Since the bullet was damaged too bad to make a perfect match, we'll have to be satisfied with that."

"I'm going to see William Thompson right after this. I'll let you know what happens with the interview," Levi said, pushing himself to his feet and donning his cowboy hat.

"Good. I need to stay here. We still have to find the flash drive."

"If it's William behind all of this, won't the threat be over with?" Melora desperately wanted it to be true, but the doubt that entered Daniel's gaze told her otherwise.

"He might not be the only one. He may be the one behind your immediate threat, but until we discover what Axle hid, there's always a chance more can happen."

More. More than being assaulted, run off the road and terrorized. Melora's shoulders slumped as she entwined her fingers in her lap. "Then we need to expand our search to the cabana this afternoon.

The quicker we find the flash drive the quicker my life will return to normal." She almost choked on the last word. She didn't know what normal was anymore. Hadn't in over two years.

"I'll walk you out, Levi." Gisella stood, her attention trained on Melora. "We'll find out what's going on, Melora."

After Gisella left with Levi, their low murmurs wafting to Melora, she squeezed her fingers even tighter together. Pain spread up her arms until Daniel covered her clasped hands with his.

"I second what Gisella said. I'm not going to let this go until I have all the people involved."

She tried to smile, but her mouth wouldn't cooperate. The feel of his hand over hers, rubbing across hers as though he could massage the tension away, clogged her throat. He knew what to say to make her feel better. With him around she didn't feel alone, but she was so afraid she was coming to depend on him in such a short time. *What will happen when this is all over and he goes back to his other duties?*

"If William Thompson is behind this, then that means my uncle was involved. He knew what was happening to me and didn't care." There she said what had been bothering her ever since she'd heard William's name in connection with Clyde Walker. What little comfort she'd drawn from Daniel's touch vanished, stress locking her muscles in place.

"We don't know the extent of your uncle's involve-ment."

Her gaze latched on to his as if it were a safety net. She wanted to believe her uncle, who had raised her since she was eight, didn't know anything about the danger to her personally. She started to say something when the phone ringing cut through the quiet. Gasping, she flinched.

"I can get it," Daniel said.

She shook her head and reached for the phone on the end table by the couch. She needed to deal with her problems. All too soon, Daniel would leave, and she would have to face the wreck her life had become.

"Hello."

"Melora, this is Juanita," said a quiet, raspy voice, that didn't sound at all like her housekeeper.

TWELVE

Something's wrong. "Juanita?" Melora said to let Daniel know who was calling.

Daniel withdrew his cell and made a call, signaling her to keep Juanita on the line.

"Don't bother trying to trace this. It's a throwaway phone. I had to call you. I couldn't disappear without letting you know I'm okay. I owe you that at least." Juanita's voice grew a little stronger as she talked.

"Why did you leave?" Melora could remember all the times Juanita had helped her, been her friend, listened to her.

"Because they killed Señor Madison."

"They? Who?" Melora's gaze linked with Daniel's.

"Don't know. Don't wanna know." A long pause, then Juanita continued in a husky voice as though tears welled up in her throat. "I'm so sorry for everything. I shouldn't have spied on you for Señor Madison."

"Spied on me?" The words tumbled from her mouth as though her tongue didn't quite work.

Daniel slid closer to her on the couch and placed his arm along the back cushion. His nearness helped to alleviate the betrayal swamping her at Juanita's confession.

"Yes, that's why I came to work for you. He wanted to make sure you were all right. And then when your husband died, he wanted to know how you were doing, what was going on, especially after that break-in two years ago."

"He knew about it?"

"Yes, and he told me not to worry. He'd take care of it. Then everything settled down until recently. I didn't understand all that was going on until I talked with my sister. She told me Señor Madison was part of a powerful group of people called the Lions of Texas. She heard him arguing with one of them over the phone the morning he was killed."

"About what?" Melora couldn't keep her hand holding the phone from trembling.

"He demanded they leave you alone. That he'd find the flash drive. If not, they would regret it. When he was killed, she thought we might be next because we helped Señor Madison in the past."

"Does Carmen know who these people are?"

"She only knows two of them from when they

came to the house to talk with Señor Madison after Axle's death, but she won't even tell me who they are."

"Were they the ones who killed Axle?"

"I don't know. But Señor Madison mentioned Axle paid for trying to double-cross them. That the flash drive probably was destroyed by now. That if it hadn't turned up in two years it wouldn't now."

Had Axle collected information on a flash drive to use against the Lions of Texas to get a bigger share of the drug money? Perhaps Axle had tried to get rid of it when he was confronted by the person who killed him. If it was somewhere at the animal rescue center, the elements would have destroyed it by now.

"Carmen's scared. So am I, but we'll be safe for now. Don't try to find us. It won't do any good. Please be careful. Trust no one. I wanted you to know that Señor Madison wanted me to tell him if you found a flash drive hidden by your husband or anything else I thought might be important."

"Did he tell you what was on the flash drive?"

"He never said anything to me."

Sweat drenched her palm that held the phone. "Please come back. Daniel can protect you."

"No one can. The Lions of Texas are too powerful. I heard what happened at Señor Madison's funeral. These people are desperate, and he isn't there to protect you anymore. Carmen said he was so upset when he found out that the Texas Rangers were protecting you." Tears choked her voice.

For a long moment silence greeted Melora. She thought Juanita hung up. "Juanita, are you still there?"

"Yes," she said on a sob. "I'm so sorry. Bye, Melora."

The line went dead. Dead like so many people she'd cared about at one time. The phone slipped from her nerveless fingers and fell to her lap.

"What did Juanita say?"

Daniel's deep voice brought her back to the present. She angled toward him, his familiar scent surrounding her in comfort. "She spied on me for Uncle Tyler. Juanita said that my uncle was mixed up in the Lions of Texas. Carmen has seen two of them meeting with him at his house, but Juanita says she won't talk. I think my talking to you got my uncle killed."

He covered her trembling hands in her lap. "Your uncle was involved with some bad people. You did the right thing by confiding in me and getting help. This is too big for you alone to deal with. You have Kaitlyn to think about."

Yes, she had to remember that. Her uncle had made his choice when he had joined a group of criminals.

Daniel's cell rang, and he answered it. "Thanks,

Evan. It was worth a try." He hung up. "They couldn't trace the call."

"She told me it couldn't be traced and not to come looking for her. They were in a safe place. Is there such a place?"

"It's not as easy to disappear as it used to be, but it can be done." He settled his hand on her shoulder, comforting, supporting. "Are you all right?"

"No. I don't know what to feel anymore. There are times I feel numb and other times I feel overwhelmed with emotions. Mostly I feel betrayed, especially by Uncle Tyler. But Juanita thinks I'm alive because he protected me. He probably convinced the Lions of Texas after they searched my house two years ago and didn't find the flash drive, that he could control the situation. He'd know if a flash drive turned up and could take care of it for them. Then Axle's body was found and you all got involved in the case. They must have felt I was enough of a threat that they would go against one of their members. So now what?"

"Find the information they will kill for. And why do they think you know where it is?"

"Then we should start immediately at the cabana. I haven't been there much since Axle's death. He used to throw swimming parties at the house and used it a lot then."

"With our hot summers, you haven't used the pool since your husband died?"

"Kaitlyn and I swim, but we never go into the cabana." Like the office, she thought of the place as Axle's domain. Suddenly, she sat forward. "What we're looking for just might be out there. I forgot all about how much Axle liked to spend time there, especially in the summer. It was set up mostly for entertaining, but he might have hidden something there."

"Good. That'll give us something to do while Levi brings Thompson in for questioning. There's also some other leads concerning Clyde Walker that need to be tracked down."

Something in his tone caused Melora to pause in rising and look at him. "Does it bother you that you're here protecting me and Kaitlyn rather than out rounding up the suspects?"

The intensity in his expression zeroed in on her. "No. This is the place I need to be. I have capable Rangers working on the case with me. I don't have to do everything myself."

"Mommy?"

Melora's gaze swung toward the entrance into the living room. With one hand Kaitlyn knuckled the sleep out of her eyes and with the other she clutched Mr. Snuggles. "Hi, honey."

"Where's Gisella?" Kaitlyn wandered over to Melora and sat between her and Daniel. "She promised me she would help me make Christmas cookies today."

"She did?" So many things had been happening lately that she felt her life careening out of control as if she were racing down a mountain with no brakes.

Kaitlyn exaggerated a nod, hugging the stuffed dog against her chest. "You can help, too."

Melora glanced at Daniel over the top of her daughter's head. "Can I help with decorating them after you two bake them? Daniel and I have to clean out the cabana."

Kaitlyn wrinkled her nose. "That place stinks."

Melora started to say, "It does?" when she remembered one of the reasons she didn't like the cabana. Axle had smoked and the place always smelled of cigarettes. "Today isn't too cold so I'm going to air it out some."

"Good or you'll stink, too."

"Ah, there you are, Kaitlyn. I was in the kitchen making sure we had everything for the cookies. Are you ready?" Gisella stood in the living room entrance.

"Yeah," Kaitlyn said with enthusiasm, then kissed Melora on the cheek then Daniel, whose eyes widened.

A grin split his face. "Thanks, Gisella. You've gone above and beyond your duty."

The female Ranger winked at them. "Just find what we need to nab these people."

Daniel chuckled. "I guess we'd better get down

to business before they rope us into making cookies." Rising, he held out his hand.

The contact with his palm brought back all the reasons she needed to steel herself against Daniel's charm. She'd trusted several people who all let her down. She couldn't do that again. Although she knew Daniel would keep her safe as possible physically, what about emotionally? Her heart was already connected to him, and she was afraid when that link was severed, the hurt would overshadow all that had happened in the past few years.

Beyond the large window at the front of the cabana the dim shadows of twilight settled over the pool area. After shutting the window, Melora pulled the blinds closed and instantly the large room seemed to shrink to half its size. As she panned the area, disappointment weaved through her. They had found nothing. Where could Axle have put the information? What had made him stop wearing the flash drive around his neck and possibly hide it? If it wasn't one of the Lions of Texas, who was his killer? A rival drug gang?

"What if there wasn't anything that Axle hid. That this is all a big joke on us—on the people he crossed?" she asked Daniel.

"After we've checked everywhere, we might need to consider that. But either way the people who want it certainly don't want us to get to it first. Where do you think we should look tomorrow?"

Frustrated, Melora flittered her hand in the air. "I'm running out of places." She skimmed the room as though it could reveal some hidden cache she'd previously forgotten. They'd checked the baseboards and for any loose tiles in the floor. They'd examined the walls, especially behind the pictures. She stopped at one arrangement of photographs that Axle had taken. Several were of his champion Arabian horse and the others were of his dog that had died about six months before Axle. He'd loved both of those animals to the point she'd felt more than she.

She marched across the cabana and took down one photo of the black gelding in the pasture behind the stable. Although she had neighbors on both sides of her several hundred yards away, the property went back several acres. Tearing into the back of the picture, she stripped away the paper, hoping there was something hidden there. Nothing. She moved on to the next photo and finally finished several minutes later with Daniel pausing in packing up the last box and peering at her.

"I'm desperate, okay?"

He closed the space between them and stacked the photos on top of each other. "Actually that wasn't a bad idea. He could have hidden something behind one."

"Yeah, that's what I was hoping, but as you can see, that wasn't the case." She lifted the top picture of Axle's hunting dog, Bailey. "He loved this animal so much he had him buried at the back of the property. Has a headstone and everything. He used to go out and put flowers on the grave every Sunday afternoon." She bit back, "he loved that dog more than me," but it was the truth.

"Every week?"

"Yeah."

Daniel pointed to the picture of the Arabian horse. "I've been down to the stable. I didn't see this horse."

"I sold him about a year ago. I have a horse for myself and Kaitlyn that a neighbor's been helping me care for, but his stallion was high-strung and didn't like anyone but Axle. My husband used to spend a lot of time with him."

"Then let's check both the stable and the gravesite out. We're running out of places and since he spent time at both those places, we should take a good hard look at them."

"Most of Lightning's riding gear went with him. His stall is empty though."

"Okay, then first thing tomorrow that's where we'll start."

A knock sounded at the door. Daniel whirled around at the same time she did. He frowned and hurried to answer it.

"Clay, what are you doing here?" Daniel asked, surprise flashing across his face.

"I heard about what happened at Tyler Madison's funeral. Someone said a Ranger got hurt. I…" Clay's gaze swung to Melora then back to his dad.

Melora came up beside Daniel. "One of the Rangers guarding the back door was knocked out, but he's fine now. I'm Melora Hudson." She held out her hand.

Clay shook it. "Nice to meet you."

"How did you know where I was?" Surprise still lit his eyes as though Daniel couldn't believe his son was standing in front of him.

"The internet," Clay said as if that were a no-brainer.

"Well, since you've come all this way, I hope you'll stay for dinner. We'll have pizza." Melora stepped to the side to let the young man inside.

"Sure." Clay peered around the cabana with some cartons piled in the center of the room. "What are you doing in here?"

"I needed help boxing up my deceased husband's belongings. Your dad has been gracious enough to help."

"Yeah, he's that kinda guy." Clay's look seared into his dad. "Why didn't you call and let me know you were all right?"

"I wasn't hurt. I didn't think about it. I've been

so busy with this case that…" Daniel plowed his fingers through his hair. "I'm sorry. I should have. I know you get worried when you hear about a Ranger getting hurt."

A nerve in Clay's jaw twitched. "This was a mistake." He spun around and trod toward the back door into the kitchen.

"Score points for my side. Not." Daniel shook his head and started toward the house. "Maybe I can catch him."

Melora stepped out into the cool night air. "Maybe it's about time he realizes what kind of job you have."

"It's a little late to do a ride along."

"Have you ever talked to him about your job?"

"He used to ask questions when he was younger, but so much I couldn't talk about. He was too young and didn't need to hear about the evil in this world."

"Well, he isn't anymore. You've helped so many people. Me, for one." At the back door, she stopped Daniel from entering with a hand on his arm. "He came all the way out here because he was worried about you. Remember that when you talk to him. He's made a move. Now it's your turn. He needs to be treated like the adult he's becoming."

When Daniel entered, he came to a halt a few feet into the kitchen.

"I baked these." Kaitlyn was showing Clay the Christmas cookies she decorated. "On this one, I wanted to make it sparkle like a Christmas tree."

"I think you did. It's beautiful."

Melora smiled at the huge grin on her daughter's face as Kaitlyn puffed out her chest. "You can have it." She gave Clay the cookie shaped like a tree with every color of glittery sparkles sold at their local grocery store on it. "We're having pizza. We can't have any cookies until after dinner."

"I'm not staying—" Clay glanced at his dad then back at Kaitlyn. "What kind of pizza?"

"The best. Pepperoni."

"I guess I can stay for a little while."

Later that evening Clay snatched another Christmas cookie off the plate sitting on the coffee table in the den and said, "It's your turn."

Melora lined up for her shot at the trash can across the room. Compressing the ball of paper in her hands even more, she squinted and took aim. The wad sailed across the distance and plopped right down next to the "basket."

"Yay!" Kaitlyn jumped up and down then gave Clay a high five before doing a little dance in a circle, singing, "We won! We won!"

Laughing, Clay did a jig then took a bite of his cookie.

Melora sidled toward Daniel and out of the

corner of her mouth said in a low whisper, "Some people need to learn how to win gracefully."

"Your daughter is competitive. Like her mother."

"When I agreed to this little game of paper basketball, I didn't realize how hard it would be to hit the basket. I understand about your son making most of his shots, but where did my daughter learn to do it? And why aren't you better at the game?"

Daniel grinned. "I'm not the one who missed the tying shot."

When Kaitlyn started to grab her fourth cookie in the past hour, Melora stepped forward. "You've had enough, honey. It's time for bed. Actually it's way past your bedtime."

"Can't I stay up a little later? At least until Clay goes home."

Daniel's son tousled Kaitlyn's hair. "Sorry, half-pint. I've got to go now."

"Please stay a little longer and read me a story. I can be ready for bed fast." Kaitlyn tried to snap her fingers, but it didn't work.

"Okay. One story. If you can be ready in five minutes."

At Clay's challenge, Kaitlyn raced out of the den, the sound of her pounding steps echoing down the upstairs hallway.

"Thanks, Clay. I thought I was going to have a

rebellion on my hands." Melora was so glad that she'd asked Daniel's son to stay for dinner. Kaitlyn had monopolized the teen's time, but her presence had also kept the atmosphere casual and fun. Something both Daniel and Clay needed.

Gisella appeared in the doorway. "Daniel, may I have a word with you?"

"Can it wait?"

"No."

"Be back in a few minutes," Daniel said as he left the room.

Clay frowned. "Does he ever not work?"

"What was the past two hours? Work?" Melora faced the young man.

"Isn't he here because he's working a case?"

She put a hand on her waist. "Yes, and because of your father, I'm alive. He saved my life yesterday. I'd say he's doing a pretty good job. Your father is one of the people who helps keep us safe. If it weren't for people like him, what do you think would happen in this world?"

"He works all the time."

"Yes, I agree his job takes a lot of his time. But for a relationship to work, it takes both people. I'm glad you came tonight. Daniel needed to take some time off from this case."

"Kaitlyn really likes him," Clay said as though that surprised him.

"Yes, from the first day she met him." Her

daughter wanted a father figure. Melora could see that and wasn't sure what to do about it because Daniel's life did revolve around his job. In that moment, she realized she was falling in love with him. The realization shocked her into silence.

"He can have that effect on some people."

"But not you?"

"We tend to end up arguing more than anything."

"You could change that pattern."

"Why are you interested?"

"Because I care about your father. As I said, I'm alive because of him. My daughter is. I lost my parents when I was young, and I would give anything to have them in my life now. I don't want you to end up regretting your relationship when you get older and maybe don't have a chance to be with your dad."

"He has a funny way of showing he cares. He's always telling me what I need to do."

"When you were in trouble a few years back, who did you turn to? Who helped you out of a jam?"

Bright red blotched his face. "I still had to do community service."

"Because you did something wrong. Do you think you're so special that you don't have to follow the rules?"

"No."

"Then quit being so angry at your father for something you did. And a lot of parents feel they need to tell their kids what they should do. It's hard to let that go as they grow up. Talk to your father about how you feel. That you want to be treated as an equal now that you're seventeen."

Clay peered toward the entrance and saw Daniel standing there. "I'd better read Kaitlyn her story." He hurried out of the room.

Leaving Melora to face Daniel. His neutral expression evolved into one of anger. "I appreciate what you were trying to do, but I don't need you to fight my battles."

His words bombarded her. "So it's okay if you help me, but not the other way around?"

He glared at her, his mouth a tight line.

The intensity that flowed off him zapped what energy she had. All she wanted to do now was see that Kaitlyn got to bed then find her own. She needed to sleep, to hide from her problems for a while. To get a handle on the fact that she wasn't just falling in love with Daniel, but was in love with him. "I'm going to see to my daughter then go to bed." She headed toward him. "What did Gisella want? Any news about the case?"

"Yeah. William Thompson is gone and they've found Gordon Johnson's body about six hundred yards from where Axle was killed. He was shot like your husband."

"I was hoping with Clyde Walker's death this would all neatly wrap itself up and Kaitlyn and I could get back to a normal life."

"No, not yet, but with each piece of information we're getting closer to who killed Axle and where the flash drive is."

"I hope so," Melora said with a deep sigh, then started for Kaitlyn's room down the hall as Clay left her daughter's bedroom.

Daniel watched his son approach him, a leery look in his expression. "How's basketball going?" he asked, remembering the first game of the season four weeks ago when Clay's team got killed by their opponent.

"Better, but then you'd know if you'd come to see me more than a couple of times."

"If I remember correctly you weren't too thrilled that I came to see you that first game. After the third one you made it clear you didn't want me in the audience."

"Since when have you done what I wanted?" Clay gripped the railing of the staircase as he put his foot on the first step.

"You said I made you nervous."

Clay snorted. "Come to the tournament in a couple of days. I don't care if you're there or not."

Daniel had waited weeks to hear his son ask him

to come to a game. "I'll probably be working, but as soon as this case is over, I'll be there."

"Don't bother. You never understood how much I love the game."

Stunned, Daniel allowed his son to descend the staircase. Such anger. It still felt as though it swirled around him like a whirlwind. Suddenly shaking his head, he hurried after his son. He caught up with Clay at the front door.

"Please don't leave just yet," Daniel said as he quickly covered the length of the large foyer.

Clay placed his hand on the doorknob but didn't turn it. Although Daniel couldn't see his son's face, his stiff back and rigid set of his shoulders spoke of his anger.

"I know how important basketball is to you. I'll be at the next game I can make. I want to support you in this. I'm glad you have something that you love like you do basketball."

Clay took a half turn to the left. "You mean that?"

"Yes. If you want to pursue a career in basketball, I'll be there cheering you on when I can."

"What's caused your change of opinion?"

"I had someone remind me what it was like with my own father. He didn't want me to go into law enforcement. We fought about it, and it came between us. I never got the chance to clear the air with him before he died. I don't want that for us."

Clay's eyes narrowed as though he were mulling over what Daniel had said. "I'll send you my schedule. Come when you can. Good night, Dad."

Unsure where he stood with his son, Daniel started to call him back. Seeing the two Rangers patrolling the grounds locked the words inside. This wasn't a place for his son right now. When the case was over, he would approach Clay again. Make this right somehow.

The next afternoon after spending all morning going through Lightning's old stall, the tack room and any other place in the stable Daniel thought might contain something Axle would want to hide, Melora exited Daniel's white truck not far from where Bailey was buried. She was glad the driveway split off and circled the back of the property because after spending another sleepless night she didn't have much energy left to walk all the way to the gravesite.

A small grove of trees shaded the dog's burial place. She stopped not far from it. Since her husband's disappearance, the grass surrounding the grave had grown up around it and because it was December, had died leaving long brown growth tangled about the stone. Axle would never have allowed that to happen.

"You say he took care of this every week?" Daniel stood over the headstone, staring down at it.

"Like clockwork. Every Sunday afternoon. I only mentioned this place to you because he did, but I can't see there being anywhere to hide something. It's not like he would have dug up Bailey and put something in the coffin."

"Coffin?"

"My husband loved his animals more than people. He treated them better, too."

Daniel knelt and checked out the pop-up vase standing at the bottom of the stone with Bailey's name etched into it. "Nothing here but very old remains of some stems." He picked one up and it fell apart, the pieces plunging to the ground at his feet. When he peered up, his gaze lit on the photo display that latched on to the headstone. "Is that Bailey?"

"Yes. A smaller version of one of the pictures in the cabana."

"Your husband didn't spare any expense with Bailey's burial."

"That was Axle. He loved to spend money. I know the restaurants were doing well, but I sometimes wondered about his extravagances. Now I know he supplemented his income by illegal means."

Daniel rose and bent over to examine the photo display. The back popped open to slip a picture into the holder. Before he could look inside, his phone blared in the quiet December afternoon. Daniel quickly answered it.

He turned his back on Melora and walked a few paces away. She watched his posture stiffen, his spine ramrod straight as he clutched the phone to his ear. The low rumble of his voice drifted to her, but she couldn't make out what was being said.

They had spent all morning together searching the stable, but the barrier he'd erected between them last night over Clay had grown until she didn't think she could scale it. He was determined to shut her out. Just like Axle had. So she'd come to the conclusion that they weren't meant to be together. Hence the sleepless night trying to rid herself of any feelings she had for Daniel. She hadn't been successful. She loved him. Whereas it had taken her over a year to fall in love with Axle, in two weeks' time she'd fallen for Daniel—hard.

Daniel walked back toward her. His frown deepened.

"What happened? More bad news?" Melora steeled herself for another setback. The news of William Thompson's disappearance last night had been a blow. She'd wanted him to break down and tell the Texas Rangers everything so she could get back to her normal life.

"Thompson was traced to a country with no extradition agreement."

"So he's alive and skipped the country. I would say that is an admission of guilt."

"But it makes questioning him very hard. Levi has asked a judge for a warrant to search his office and home for any evidence. Maybe Thompson left something behind to help us."

"But you don't think so?"

"He's had a while to cover his tracks—ever since we requested the paperwork involving the restaurant chain. I doubt this was a spur of the moment getaway."

"Great. We're right back where we started with a lot of questions and no answers." Tired, overwhelmed by all the dead ends, Melora leaned against the headstone, staring down at the photo of Bailey. "What do we do now?"

"I'm going to finish checking this gravesite out then we'll go back and get Gisella's input on where to look next." Daniel approached her and slipped the whole photograph display off the headstone, then opened the back of it. He fished around in the box-like container and withdrew something wrapped in a waterproof covering. After peeling it away, he revealed a flash drive. "Bingo."

THIRTEEN

Back at the house, Daniel connected the flash drive to the computer in the office and waited for the files to pop up on the screen. Behind him stood Melora, her spicy scent reminding him of the cinnamon rolls he used to love when he was a child. "I hope this will give us some answers."

As a series of initials and numbers came up on the monitor, Melora shook her head. "This doesn't make any sense. What do they mean?"

"It's got to be some kind of code Axle had."

"Leave it to Axle not to make things simple." Daniel chuckled. "The story of my life."

Melora leaned closer, over his shoulder and pointed at the letters BHTX. "TX for Texas?"

For a few seconds his concentration deviated from the information. He swung his head toward Melora. Their gazes met. Her nearness stole his breath until the sound of his cell ringing cut into the silence hovering between them.

He fumbled for his phone and said, "Riley here."

"I'm at the hospital guarding Quin today," Oliver said after he identified himself. "I thought I would let you know that it looks like he might wake up soon. He's been moving more than usual. The doctors are optimistic."

"Good. If he does, call me immediately. I can be there in half an hour."

"I'll let you know if there's a change."

After Daniel hung up and set his cell down next to the computer, he glanced toward Melora who had backed away several feet, an unreadable expression on her face. "Quin might be waking up. If he does, I'd like you to be there when I talk with him. Maybe your presence will help loosen his tongue."

"I'll do anything to end this." She kept her distance as though regretting her nearness earlier.

He forced his attention away from her and on the screen. "A lot of these have initials that end in TX. It's reasonable to think TX means Texas. If that's the case we can start by seeing what towns start with the first letters."

"It could be a business name."

"Yeah or a person. All possibilities will have to be tracked down."

"And the numbers? An address or phone number?"

"Or latitude and longitude. Or the amount of a shipment going in or out. There are a lot of possibilities."

"In other words, days and days of more work tracking down all the leads."

He heard the deflated tone in her voice and wanted to reassure her that it would come to an end soon, but he wouldn't give her false hope. "We'll do our best." He continued to scan through the numbers and initials until close to the end of the document. A series of notes glared off the bright screen—a few that were obvious what they meant—some couched in vague words that left him even more puzzled.

Melora moved closer again and touched the computer monitor. "Uncle Tyler wasn't Axle's partner, but his boss. And this one confirms William Thompson was involved with both of them. This is worse than I thought. My uncle betrayed me from the beginning. I kept hoping he didn't know what was happening with Axle." Her disbelief evolved into anger. If the three men in question had walked through the door at that moment, the glare from her eyes would have struck them down.

"Axle brought the drugs into the country, then your uncle took over from there. I don't think Tyler trusted Axle totally. All the references to the distributors are vague as though Axle didn't know who they were, only bits and pieces."

"Why did Axle write all this down?"

"For insurance? Axle didn't trust Tyler, either? Axle was trying to figure it all out to make a move against your uncle? We may never know exactly."

"No honor among drug runners." Her mouth pressed in a tight line, she pointed at the screen. "Look at that reference."

"Tyler's contact at Mercy continues to be the best distributor in the area."

"Mercy Hospital? Where I volunteer?"

"Where Quin is. Possibly. A hospital and drugs certainly go together."

"What's that number at the end of the sentence mean?"

"Good question. A room number, an extension number for the contact?" Daniel printed the document then closed it on the computer.

"Maybe a room number, but not the other. They all start with 7."

He gathered up the sheets after they printed. "If it's Mercy. I think the best way to find out is to check the place out. See what this number gives me."

"I'm coming with you." He started to protest her involvement when she hurriedly added, "I know the hospital and the people who work there. I might be able to help."

He frowned. "You should stay here."

"Why? I'm safe with you. I've got to do something. I feel so helpless. That way Gisella only has to worry about Kaitlyn."

Shaking his head, he scooted the chair back from the desk. "I'm only agreeing because I think you can help. And while we're there, we'll stop by and see if anything is happening with Quin. Besides, knowing you, you'd probably follow me."

"I'd rather ride with you." She gave him an impish smile that tempted him to forget he wasn't the kind of man she needed.

"Fine. Let's find Gisella and tell her what we're doing."

Melora headed out of the office several steps in front of him. Determination marked her action, her arms stiff at her sides. Although they'd found the flash drive, she would never be safe until he figured out who had killed her husband. Had it been her uncle all along? Even if it was him, who had hired Walker to come after her family?

Gisella and Kaitlyn were in the den, trying to coax Patches out from under the couch.

Gisella straightened up when she saw Melora and Daniel coming into the room. "What's up?"

"We're going to Mercy Hospital to check some things out." While Melora covered the space between her and Kaitlyn, Daniel drew Gisella out into the hallway and handed her the printed pages and the flash drive. "I'll have Anderson come pick this up. I think we found the information everyone has been looking for."

Gisella flipped through several pages. "What in the world does BHTX mean or GATX? Something in Texas?"

"Probably. That's what we'll need to figure out."

"I see BHTX is in here several times."

"Yeah, I noticed a couple of initials were."

"Is this everything on the flash drive?" Gisella thumbed the sheaf of paper she held.

"Yes, pages of initials and numbers and references to the network Tyler Madison and Axle set up. One being a contact at Mercy."

"And you think it is the hospital?"

"Could be. While I'm checking out the hospital, see what else Mercy might be."

"I know of a Mercy Assisted Living Center not far from where I live. I'll track down a list of other places."

"Great. Give me a call when you have it."

As Gisella went back into the den, Melora came out of the room. "Kaitlyn finally got Patches out from under the couch. With all that has happened lately, that cat might need a pet psychologist."

Making his way down the stairs, he slid a glance toward her. "There is such a thing?"

She shrugged. "It wouldn't surprise me. Look at the extremes Axle went to for his dog. I also knew a friend of my uncle's who used to send her cat on a vacation to a five-star pet hotel once a year."

After settling into his truck, Daniel placed a call to Anderson to let him know about the flash drive, then to his captain to give him an update. By the time he completed his second call, they were halfway to the hospital.

"If it is someone at Mercy Hospital, do you think Quin is safe, especially if he wakes up?" Melora asked, drawing his attention at a stoplight. "He may know who the person at the hospital is. What if my uncle was about to tell me something and was silenced?"

"Walker wasn't hired to kill you, but your uncle? Looking into Walker's background and his training as a sniper, I wouldn't doubt that at all." He pulled into the parking lot at the hospital. "We'll check Quin first then look for the number."

Five minutes later, Daniel and Melora stepped off the elevator. He scouted the area, searching for anything unusual. Normal activity hummed around him, staff going about their duties. "Let's go." Taking Melora's hand, he hurried toward room 414. "I'll just stick my head in to see what's going on with Quin and let Oliver know we're in the hospital."

Daniel settled his hand on the handle and thrust the door open to Quin's room. Not seeing Oliver, he took a couple of steps inside. Something hard came down on his head. The room spun before his eyes. Right before darkness swallowed him up, he heard Melora scream.

Melora followed Daniel into the coma man's room a few steps behind him. She saw him crumble to the floor. The sight produced a scream that erupted from her mouth.

Right before she swung her attention to Jorge holding the barrel of a gun as though he'd used it to strike Daniel.

Her gaze latched on to Jorge's security badge and noticed his ID number was 5389, the same numbers that were written down next to the sentence about Mercy on Axle's flash drive. She tried to back out of the open doorway, sounds of running footsteps coming down the hall behind her. Jorge's wide gaze took in what was happening in the corridor. He quickly covered the space between her and grabbed her, plastering her against his chest.

"Don't try anything stupid, Melora, or I'll kill you." He moved out into the hallway, the gun pressed to her temple. "Get back or I'll shoot her. Now!" he shouted to the people responding to her scream.

They all stepped away and gave Jorge room to escape. Dragging Melora with him, he headed toward the elevator.

* * *

Daniel heard voices coming from the corridor. A man shouting, someone weeping. He willed his eyes to open although his head throbbed, pain threatening to push him back into the dark void.

He blinked and focused on a nurse bending over him. "What happened?"

"Dr. Cantana has taken Melora as a hostage. He went to the elevator."

Struggling to sit up, the room spinning, Daniel managed with the nurse's help to get to his elbows and survey the area. Oliver lay on the floor off to the side out of the view of anyone coming into 414. Another nurse was tending to his friend. Daniel's gaze swept to Quin in the bed. The monitor indicated he was still alive, and for a second he allowed relief to flutter through him as he tried to think clearly.

Then the words the nurse had just said fully registered. *Dr. Cantana has taken Melora*. He pushed himself up farther. Swayed. Nearly collapsed back to the floor. He didn't have time to be wounded. He bit down hard and drudged up all the willpower he had to stand. Finally, he rose slowly. Each second it took him eroded his patience.

Melora's life was in danger. He'd promised her he would keep her safe.

"We need to lock down the hospital, call the

police and the Texas Rangers," he said to the head of security for the hospital who had burst into the room as Daniel got his bearings.

The nurse who bent over Oliver said, "He's alive."

"Was he hit?" Daniel asked while the pounding of his head amplified all the noise around him. But at least the room wasn't swaying as a doctor rushed into it.

"I don't see any kind of head trauma or gunshot wound," the nurse said.

The doctor knelt next to Oliver, spied something under the bed and reached for it. He held up a syringe, empty of any contents. "Becky, I need this analyzed stat."

More medical help arrived. Daniel pulled the security chief out into the hallway to allow the doctors and nurses to work on Oliver. "We need to check the hospital security cameras to see where Dr. Cantana is taking Melora."

"Come this way."

As Daniel made his way to the security office, he received a call from Evan. "I'm going to check the cameras then start looking. Coordinate a floor-to-floor search with the police."

"I'm pulling into the parking lot."

Daniel disconnected as he and the security chief entered his office. Had they locked down the hospital fast enough?

* * *

Sweat drenched Melora, more from fear than the stifling heat in the basement. "Why are you doing this?" She slowed her pace, hoping to delay Jorge as much as possible. Was Daniel all right? Did Daniel know what happened to her?

"I've got to get out of here. You're my ticket out of the hospital."

She'd seen security cameras mounted in certain strategic locations about the building, but few were on this bottom floor and none in the stairwell they'd used. "They know you're the person they're after. Give yourself up. I'm sure you can make a deal with the authorities to testify against the people—"

"Shut up." Jorge grabbed her, his fingers digging into her arm. "Don't you understand what they do to people who cross them? Your husband is dead. He tried to get a bigger slice than he was supposed to. They don't take kindly to that. I've messed up, and they won't be pleased with me. I couldn't even kill Quin. You and that Ranger had to come in and let the whole floor know."

"Who are they?" The wild-eyed look, like a trapped animal forced to fight to the end, Jorge gave her unnerved her.

"Your uncle is dead because he was going soft. Wanted to protect you at all cost. They couldn't trust him or you any longer. And they couldn't afford for the information Axle had complied to be found. Your uncle and I were given the task of finding Axle's info. He threatened them. *Them.* Axle was insane to think he should get a bigger cut of the action." Shoving her forward, he waved her along with the gun. "Keep moving. If I get out of here, I'll be able to get away. I've planned for this. I have enough money stashed to disappear where no one will find me."

"Where are we going?"

"I'm hoping they haven't thought about this back entrance into the building. If they have, then I have you to get me out of here. I saw how that Ranger was hovering over you at your uncle's funeral. He's not going to let anything happen to you. I'm counting on his cooperation if he wants to see you alive again." His voice went from frantic to icy as though he were finally getting enough control over his fear to do what he needed to get away.

She needed to come up with a way to escape. "There's always Witness Protection."

He laughed, a high-pitched sound. "I have my family to think about. I'm not going to be taken, Melora."

Alive. He hadn't said that word, but that was what he meant. She heard it in his voice. She saw it in the resolve in his expression as she glanced back at him. "Did you kill Axle?"

"Clyde Walker did. Axle and his bodyguard both. Your uncle ordered it."

The feeling of betrayal multiplied, and she had to resist the urge to give into it. Not now. She had to remain as calm as possible if she wanted to stay alive. "But you hired Clyde Walker to carry out the hit two years ago."

"Yes, but I didn't have anything to do with the death of your uncle. They did. They should have found someone else. Clyde was becoming unpredictable. I suspected he was taking drugs, but I needed someone fast and he'd done a good job in the past. He was just supposed to frighten you so you wouldn't say anything to the police."

Listening to Jorge tell her what he'd done made her realize she wouldn't get out of this alive unless she did something about it. Jorge wasn't going to let her go when he got away from the hospital. She knew too much, and this man she'd known for years was losing it.

Before she turned the next corner, Jorge gripped her arm and hauled her back against him. The barrel of the gun poked into her back, doubling her already fast heart rate.

Lord, help me. What do I do?

Walking in sync with Jorge, Melora rounded the corner at the end of the dim corridor and came to a halt. Furniture stacked against the wall and door blocked the exit.

A curse exploded from Jorge's lips, singeing her ears with his fury. Sounds coming from the hallway they had used reverberated through the air. Footfalls.

Thoughts of a shootout made her stumble as Jorge shoved her toward the furniture, his gaze darting back the way they came. She fell against a desk, toppling a chair to the cement floor. The loud crash sent panic through her as her gaze flew to Jorge's enraged face.

Suddenly, Melora felt as trapped as Jorge must feel.

Watching Jorge direct Melora toward the stairs on the video footage from a few minutes ago, Daniel clenched his hands at his sides, wanting to pound his fist into the doctor's face. The pale look of fear on her face tore at his composure, something he needed at the moment. "Where do you think he would go?" He'd downed several painkillers so he could function. There was no way he wasn't going to be involved in finding Melora.

"If he wants to leave, either the basement or the first floor. Otherwise, there's no way out."

"No cameras on the stairwell?"

"No. If he comes out on a floor, we'll pick him up eventually. Not every inch of the hospital is covered but enough that he'll appear on camera soon enough. All the exits have a camera on them except a couple in the basement that aren't used anymore."

"Would Dr. Cantana know that?"

"Maybe. It isn't a secret, but it isn't broadcast, either." The security chief pointed to the bank of computers with different live pictures of the hospital. "The police have arrived."

"Good. Have them help your guards make sure all the exits are covered adequately then start a floor-by-floor search for Jorge and Melora. If you see where they are, let everyone know. I'll be in the basement. Get a team down there as fast as you can. Do you have a floor plan of that area?"

"Yeah." The man punched several keys on a computer, and the schematics came up on a screen.

With the picture in his mind of Melora's pale face as she went where she was told, Daniel studied the layout of the basement then shot out of the security office, on the cell with Levi to get his help covering that level. He couldn't stay, coordinate the search and wait for teams to report in after they check out their assigned floor. Besides, if he were Jorge, he would go to the basement.

After stepping off the elevator, Daniel paused and listened for any sounds coming from the maze of corridors in the basement. Something big hit the floor not too far away. From what he could remember, the noise came in the direction of one of the exits not used anymore.

As he started forward, the elevator chimed behind him, and the doors opened to reveal Levi and Evan. They hurried off, their expression set in grim lines, their guns in their hands.

"Which way?" Levi asked in a low voice.

"I'll take this corridor. I heard something coming from that way. There's an exit at the end of this hall. Evan, you go down that one. There's a door leading to a loading dock about halfway down it." Daniel gestured toward a hallway leading in the opposite direction. "Levi, you take that one." Daniel swung his arm around to indicate a passageway to the left. "It leads to the same exit I'm heading toward but from the other way."

Daniel strode a few feet, stopped and turned back. "Don't forget Jorge Cantana has a gun and a hostage. We have to think about her safety above anything else."

Then cautiously he covered the length of the dimly lit corridor, checking any room that opened on to it. As he neared the exit, he heard low murmurs and slowed his step. Plastering his back against the wall, he sidled toward the corner at the end of the passageway. If he remembered correctly, the door to the outside was only a few yards away on the opposite wall.

* * *

"Move faster." Jorge said in a furious whisper.

With his weapon trained on her, Melora tried to do what he told her, but her sweaty hands trembled so badly her grip kept slipping on the wood. A chair lay at her feet and the anger that encompassed Jorge's face scared her more than the gun pointed at her. She'd never seen him like this before.

"If I go down, you're going down with me. You're the reason everything has fallen apart."

Jorge's low rants bombarded her ears as he thrust himself close to her. He was falling apart and there was no telling what he would do when cornered.

Melora wrapped her hands around the leg of the chair at her feet and started to lift it. A noise to her left drew her attention at the same time Jorge grabbed her and pressed her against his chest. He aimed his weapon at her head.

"Drop the gun and let her go."

Hearing a deep male voice, Melora fastened her gaze on Ranger Levi McDonnell standing in the entrance of a corridor that fed into the one where she and Jorge were. Jorge positioned himself so that Melora was between him and Levi. Jorge's tremors, the biting grasp of his hand into her arm, the metal barrel pointed at her temple only verified that he was falling apart. She didn't know how she was going to make it out alive.

"What do you take me for? I'm not letting her

go. If you come any closer, I'll shoot her. I'm not being taken in."

An almost hysterical ring to his words worried Melora more than anything. Jorge was losing any rational grip he had earlier. What could she do to end this without anyone getting killed?

FOURTEEN

Daniel peered around the corner and saw Levi in front of Jorge with Melora clasped against the doctor. The pair was a couple of yards away. If he could sneak up behind the doctor, he might be able to disable him before he got a shot off. Although he could try and shoot him from this angle, Jorge might move or the bullet could go through him and hit Melora. He couldn't risk it.

He removed his shoes so he could be completely silent on the cement floor. Then he rounded the corner. Levi's gaze flicked to him but so briefly that Jorge didn't pick up on his presence.

The doctor took a step back, closer toward him. "All I want to do is leave here. I won't harm her unless you try something." Jorge kept his gaze glued to Levi, but he took another pace backward, trying to angle himself toward the wall. "I need the furniture taken down so I can leave. If you want to keep her safe, you'll start moving it."

As Daniel cut the distance between him and

Jorge, his heartbeat increased. From a well of past training, he willed himself to remain calm and composed.

A couple of more feet.

Daniel turned his gun in his hand so he could use it to knock Jorge out. Every nerve taut with tension, he crept even closer, praying to the Lord that the doctor didn't suddenly decide to glance behind him.

"You aren't going to get away. The police are all over the place and the grounds," Levi said in a professional negotiator's voice, keeping Jorge's attention on him. "I can move the furniture, but do you really think you can escape?"

"Yeah, with Melora. She's my guarantee."

Daniel raised the butt of the gun and in one quick move brought it down on Jorge's head. The man jerked, then collapsed to the floor while Levi rushed forward and Melora stumbled and went down, too.

"I'll take care of him," Levi said as he stooped next to Jorge.

Daniel was already moving toward Melora and knelt to help her. His arms wound about her and she folded herself against him. Her tears soaked his shirt. Her whole body shook.

"You're all right now. I won't let anything happen to you," he whispered against the top of her head.

* * *

Melora couldn't stop shaking. She hugged her arms around her middle. Her teeth chattered, the cold deep inside her bones. Looking around the staff hospital lounge, she wasn't even sure how she got up there from the basement. Daniel had deposited her in a stuffed chair, said a few soothing words to her before he was called away. She knew a Ranger stood guard outside the door. She wanted to go home. Hold her daughter and never let her go.

Hadn't Daniel said something about the guard being a precaution until they sorted everything out about what went down today?

Another betrayal swamped her as she thought back over what had happened with Jorge. He had been involved with her uncle and husband in some kind of drug-running operation. Lies were all those people had ever told her. She'd cared for each one of them, including Juanita and Alicia. Three were dead now, one being held by the police and the other in hiding all because of the Lions of Texas.

Who could she trust when she couldn't believe in her judgment anymore?

All the emotions—anger, sadness, disbelief— twisted around inside her mind, shutting down her thoughts as they overwhelmed her. Burying her face in her hands, she sucked in one shallow breath after another, but nothing seemed to fill her lungs with enough oxygen.

Kneading her fingers into her temple, she lifted her head and listened to someone talking outside the room. For a few seconds fear pushed all other feelings into the background as she relived the past hour in her mind—all in a flash.

The door opened. She captured her next inhalation and didn't release it until she saw Daniel come through the entrance. His gaze fell on to her, and a smile deep in his eyes erased the tired lines on his face.

"How are you holding up?" Tenderness laced each word.

Melora wanted to respond to the caring in his expression, but after all that had happened she couldn't afford to. "Am I free to go home?"

Two strides and he hovered over her, holding out his hand for her to take. "Yes. I'll drive you."

"If you need to stay, I can find another way."

"No. Levi is wrapping everything up. He'll see to Jorge."

Just the thought of the man who had been her daughter's doctor nauseated her. She fought the rising bile and struggled to her feet, ignoring Daniel's offered hand. She needed to do this by herself—pull her life together, depend on no one.

Melora trudged toward the hallway. When she emerged from the hospital, the sun bathed her cold body, but she didn't feel its warmth. The chill burrowed deep into her as though it had spread its tentacles over every inch of her. She pressed her folded arms closer to her chest and hurried toward Daniel's truck, refusing to acknowledge the reporters wanting a statement. What could she say to them? That her life had been built on a series of lies? Nothing had been the truth. Not her uncle's love. Not her husband's love.

She turned her head away from Daniel on the long drive to her house. She blanked her mind and stared at the passing landscape without really seeing it.

When Daniel stopped in front of her house, she opened her door before he had switched off the engine. She was halfway to her porch when he caught up with her.

He settled his hand on her shoulder. "Slow down. You should be safe now."

She whirled on him. "Safe? What's that?"

"We found the information they were after, and now it's in the hands of the authorities. We found the person behind your husband and uncle's deaths. The drug connection with your husband's restaurants has been severed."

"So you and Gisella are moving out?"

"In the next couple of days. I want to make sure all the loose ends are wrapped up."

"Then what you said about me being safe was just words uttered to appease me?"

"Well, no. But I want to be one hundred percent sure before I pull all the protection."

"Then let Gisella stay until you know one hundred percent."

He moved close, invading her personal space. Grasping her upper arms, he rubbed his hands up and down them as though that would finally chase away the cold. "Just Gisella?"

"Yes, I'm sure you have a lot of work to do, and I want my life to return to normal as quickly as possible. Kaitlyn needs that." *I need that, and if you're here it won't be.* She released a slow breath. "I'm thinking it will be best if Kaitlyn and I move away from San Antonio. Start over fresh somewhere else."

"Move away?"

She nodded, tearing her gaze from the shadows she glimpsed in his eyes.

He inched closer and drew her chin around so she could look at him. "I care about you and Kaitlyn. I was hoping we could see each other without all the intrigue. See what could develop between us. I lo—"

She pressed her fingers over his mouth, stilling his words. "Don't. It wouldn't work between us. Weren't you the one who said he wasn't comfortable being a father? Kaitlyn needs a father."

"Melora, I was wrong."

She pulled free and backed away. "Goodbye." She spun on her heels and marched toward the front porch, slipping inside the house quickly when Gisella opened the door.

While the female Ranger stepped outside, Kaitlyn ran to Melora and launched herself into her arms. Melora embraced her daughter, never wanting to let her go. The pain buried deep inside her inundated her. She loved Daniel but didn't trust her judgment anymore. What if she was wrong about him? She couldn't risk any more hurt.

In his captain's office at the Texas Ranger's office in San Antonio three days later, Daniel put his report down on Ben's desk. "It's all in there." He settled into the chair behind him.

"What did you find at Jorge's house and office?"

"A cash withdrawal from his bank account that fits with the amount Walker received right before Tyler Madison was killed, Melora's testimony about him telling her on orders from Madison he took care of Axle because he was getting greedy, the video feed that shows Jorge taking Melora hostage, and his hospital ID number is the number on the flash drive next to the reference for Mercy. We checked the lockers, room numbers and any others we could find in the hospital and that is the only match. There are a few other leads we're running down to tie him to Walker. Jorge was careful in his dealings, but Walker wasn't. I think we'll be able to build a good case against him for Axle's and the bodyguard's murders. Before it's over, we hope to tie him to the death of the maid, too."

"Good. We'll use this to see if we can get him to talk about the Lions of Texas and the drug-running operation in more detail. So far he isn't talking. I'm handing over the information to Gisella from the flash drive concerning the reference we determined was about Boot Hill, Texas. I'm sending her there to follow up on what the numbers mean. How Boot Hill fits into the drug-running operation. We know that Axle imported produce from Mexico with drugs hidden in them. How did they get across the border undetected? There are still a lot of questions involved in this case, but at least we've figured out who murdered Axle Hudson."

"And the flash drive has produced some more leads for us to follow on the distribution end." Daniel rose.

"So it was worth our time and manpower to find that information."

"Yes, now that I know Oliver will recover from the attempt to poison him." Daniel headed for the door. "We're one step closer to discovering who killed Captain Pike. I won't be satisfied until we can bring that person in and round up the whole

Lions of Texas organization." Although they had identified a few of the people, including some high-ranking ones like Tyler Madison and Jorge Cantana, Daniel was sure there were more out there and their power was far reaching.

Coming out of Ben's office, Daniel nearly ran right into Gisella. "I just heard about your new assignment in Boot Hill, Texas. When do you leave?"

"Right after Christmas. I'm going to assist the DEA in tracking down the ring working in that area."

Christmas. In a couple of days. The thought of the approaching holiday made him think about Melora and Kaitlyn. About his son. "I'm glad all that happened to Melora might produce some real leads to Captain Pike's murderer."

"So am I. I hated having to say goodbye to Kaitlyn and Melora this morning, but I'm happy they aren't in any more danger."

"How is she?"

"Kaitlyn is as cute as ever. If she has her way the house would be full of animals. She's trying to talk her mother into getting a dog for Christmas." Gisella's eyes danced with mischief.

"How about Melora?"

"Okay. She hasn't said much. She's been spending a lot of time with Kaitlyn but no one else."

He wanted to go to her, demand she let him into

her life, but after the trauma she'd been through, he needed to give her some space. And he needed to get his own life in order, which meant he had to see Clay and continue the conversation they started that evening at Melora's. "Thanks for your help with them. Have a nice holiday and keep safe in Boot Hill."

Daniel headed for the exit. His son was playing in a basketball tournament tonight, and he planned to be there in the front row. *Lord, give me the right words to make my son realize how much I love him.*

Standing in the tower room, Melora stared out the large bank of windows that gave her a view of her property and the neighbors on both sides of her. The house was totally hers again. Gisella had left a while ago. She and Kaitlyn were safe. Her life would return to normal.

A sound—not really a laugh—spilled from her mouth. Normal. What was that? She didn't think she would ever feel that again.

After three days of recuperating from the past few weeks' ordeal, she didn't feel normal. Contrary, she was more lost than before.

Because she loved Daniel. She'd thought once she got back to her house and fully realized everything was over, those feelings would die, that she'd begun to care about him because he'd kept her and Kaitlyn safe. Nothing else.

She'd been wrong. Daniel was everything Axle hadn't been.

But could she go to Daniel with the betrayals she'd experienced? How could she move on? People who had been a big part of her life had deceived her.

Lord, I need help. What do I do?

Whatever she did, she couldn't do it alone. She headed down the stairs to the second floor and her bedroom. Inside she found her Bible, sat in a chair near the window and began to read. She needed answers.

"Dad?"

Daniel pivoted toward Clay coming off the school gym floor after warm-ups. "Hi." Suddenly, he felt awkward, the words he needed to say vanishing from his mind.

"I wasn't expecting you. I thought you were tied up with that big case. I heard about what happened at the hospital and how you saved Melora."

"I've been wrapping everything up, but I wanted to see you play tonight. After the game, can we go out and talk?"

"I was gonna go out with some friends." Clay's defenses began to fall in place, a shutter closing over his expression. His body stiffened.

Daniel stepped closer in the crowd waiting for the first game in the tournament to start and lowered his voice, "Please. I have a lot to make up for."

His son blinked, surprise widening his eyes.

"I don't want our relationship to continue as it has. I love you, son."

Clay started to say something, but no words came out of his mouth. He glanced toward his coach who was signaling the players to gather in a circle around him. "I've gotta go. But I'll meet you afterward."

Daniel watched as his son and the other players bowed their heads then stacked their hands on top of each other's before breaking up with a cheer. Clay caught his gaze and gave him a half smile. Realizing he was still standing, Daniel shook the stunned sensation from himself and sat in the first row. Hope flared in him. Maybe he and Clay could work out this floundering relationship.

Leaning forward, he rested his elbows on his thighs and clasped his hands loosely together while the game started with his son as a forward. He hoped he could at least get part of his life back together. He didn't know what to do about Melora. He loved her. He wanted to be with her, but after what she said the other day he didn't think that would happen. She'd gone through so much in the past few years, and she had her daughter to think about.

"Daniel!"

He turned his head and glimpsed Kaitlyn hurrying toward him with Melora trailing behind her. When the little girl reached him, she threw her arms around him and gave him a big hug and kiss on the cheek. Daniel's heart melted at the gesture from Kaitlyn—so trusting and loving. The kiss reinforced his love for the child and her mother. Was the Lord giving him a second chance with Clay and a chance to have a wife and family, too?

"I've missed ya. Where have you been?" Kaitlyn plopped down beside him, grinning from ear to ear.

Melora stopped in front of her daughter, her green eyes clouded with uncertainty.

"Why are you two here?"

"To see Clay." Kaitlyn pointed toward his son dribbling toward the basket and making a shot. She jumped up and cheered when Clay made two points.

Melora squeezed in between Kaitlyn and the man next to her daughter on the bleachers. He graciously slid down to give her some room while Daniel did so, too. "We hit every light coming here. Kaitlyn wasn't too happy we were late."

"How did you know about the tournament?"

Daniel asked, trying to calm his heartbeat that sped at the sight of Melora.

"Clay came over to see Kaitlyn last night and invited us to see him play."

"I think Mommy wanted to come more than me." Kaitlyn swung her gaze from her mother, whose face blazed with a blush, to Daniel. "Don't tell Clay, but I made him a Christmas present."

"I'm glad you got to come to his game." Melora stared at him over the top of her daughter's head. "Clay asked a ton of questions about what happened at the hospital. He seemed interested in what you did. He read about it in the paper."

His name had been in the news the next day, and if he could have stopped that, he would have. "I was doing what I'm paid to do."

"I didn't get to thank you. I was a mess that day, but I appreciate everything you did." Although Melora's tone didn't reveal anything but politeness and gratitude, for a brief moment a look of vulnerability flickered into her expression.

"That's okay. I'm just glad it's over with."

A small smile lifted the corners of her mouth. "So am I."

"You two are supposed to be watching the game," Kaitlyn said, rolling her eyes.

"Yes, ma'am." Daniel chuckled and turned his attention toward the gym floor and his son, but as he watched the game, his gaze kept slipping toward Melora and several times he caught her looking at him.

Thank You, Lord, for giving me another chance with Clay and Melora.

"I can't believe Kaitlyn talked us into coming here." Melora peered around the large restaurant that also housed games for kids.

"According to her, she was starving, and of course, Clay is always hungry." Daniel sat back in his chair at the table for four.

"Did you see her whispering with Clay right after the game? I think they plotted this whole thing."

"But she wanted to have Clay show her how to shoot baskets."

Melora gestured toward the "basketball" game that Kaitlyn and Clay were playing now that dinner was over. "There's no court. Only balls and baskets."

Daniel laughed. "Yeah, but it's nice seeing Clay showing her how to do it."

"That's all she talked about today—getting to see Clay play tonight."

"I didn't know my son could blush, but when your daughter gave him his Christmas present then demanded he open it, he sure did."

"It's not every day a teenage guy gets a yarn

bracelet from a girl." Melora finally reconnected her gaze with Daniel's.

There was so much she wanted to say to him. After he'd left a few days ago, she'd collapsed from exhaustion—both physical and emotional. It had taken her a day to come up for air. She'd gone through the motions of living, but her thoughts had been centered on Daniel and the last look he'd given her after the incident at the hospital. She'd hurt him when he'd given her life back to her.

But not until she'd turned to the Lord in this crisis did she realize she had to trust Him, too. Yes, several people had betrayed her, but God would never betray her. He had never forsaken her as she'd thought. He would be there for her through the good, the bad and the ugly. When she finally realized that, she also knew that in order to really live she would need to take risks with her heart. Closing herself off would also close herself to love, a gift the Lord gave them.

Melora scooted to the chair next to Daniel. "I'm glad they gave us some time alone. I was so distraught that day when you brought me home. I said some things I didn't mean."

"What do you mean?"

The leeriness in his voice hurt her, but she could understand why he was feeling cautious. "After what I went through, I was questioning my judgment. I had feelings for you but was too frightened to accept them for what they are."

"What are they?"

She braced herself with a deep breath. "I love you. It's scary because I haven't known you long, but I've seen you in situations most people don't see others go through in their whole lives and your character has always been above reproach. You put Kaitlyn and me before yourself. Our safety was the most important thing to you, and I don't think it was just because it was your job."

Some of the tension in Daniel relaxed as he took her hand in his. "It's not always how long you know someone, but how well you know them. What I see in you is a wonderful mother, a caring woman who gives of herself to help others. I won't forget you were the one who listened to me about Clay and helped me to see how I can mend my relationship with my son. You're the one who told me not to give up on him. Tonight is the beginning of that." His gaze skipped to his son with Kaitlyn then back to Melora. "And for the first time in a long while I feel we have a chance at a real father/son relationship. Earlier he actually said something about spending part of Christmas with me. The last few years he's avoided that."

Twisting totally toward him, Melora cupped his jaw with her free hand. "So you think you're finally getting the hang of this father thing?"

"I may have to practice more and be reminded not to work so much, but I'm willing to give it a try. I've always liked a good challenge."

Laughter bubbled from Melora. "Well, my daughter can be a challenge if you want one."

A grin spread across his mouth and danced in his eyes. "I love you, and I want to share my life with you. I need someone to remind me of what is important."

"Your work is important."

"But not to the exclusion of the other parts of my life. You made me realize that I needed more. I don't want to end up alone with a son who doesn't want to have anything to do with me." He leaned close to her and brushed his lips across hers, then settled his mouth over hers, sealing his intentions with a kiss.

In the middle of the crowd of people in the restaurant, Melora surrendered her heart to Daniel. When they separated, their gazes trained on each other, a burst of applause sounded around them.

The heat of a blush colored her cheeks as she scanned the patrons, her attention landing on Clay and Kaitlyn, clapping with everyone else and smiling. This was the beginning of the rest of her life.

* * * * *

Dear Readers,

I loved working on this Love Inspired Suspense continuity series. I have been intrigued by the Texas Rangers for years. While researching the organization, I was impressed with their dedication and achievements. I had the honor of interviewing several Texas Rangers and they were wonderful to talk to about their work.

I love hearing from readers. You can contact me at margaretdaley@gmail.com or at P.O. Box 2074 Tulsa, OK 74101. You can also learn more about my books at http://www.margaretdaley.com. I have a quarterly newsletter that you can sign up for on my website or you can enter my monthly drawings by signing my guest book on the website.

Best Wishes,

Margaret Daley

QUESTIONS FOR DISCUSSION

1. Trust is important in a relationship. Melora didn't know whom to trust after several people betrayed her. Has anyone caused you to distrust him/her? Why? How did you settle it?

2. Who is your favorite character? Why?

3. Melora's life had become a nightmare because of her dead husband. She was scared for herself and her daughter. Have you ever been really scared? How did you deal with it?

4. Melora began to doubt that the Lord cared about her. She'd prayed for help and didn't think she was getting any from Him. Have you ever thought that? What did you do?

5. What is your favorite scene? Why?

6. Melora questioned her judgment concerning men after her marriage to Axle fell apart. Have you ever questioned your judgment about being able to read people correctly? Has it stopped you from moving forward in a relationship? What did you do to regain faith in your judgment?

7. Daniel's son, Clay, and Daniel had an estranged relationship. Daniel didn't know how to fix it. He fell back into his usual pattern of working all the time. Do you or someone you know have a similar relationship with a parent? How have you or that parent dealt with the situation?

8. Melora had a hard time telling Kaitlyn that her uncle Tyler had died. Have you ever had to tell a child a loved one died? How did you handle it?

9. Kaitlyn's life was in danger. This was hard for Melora to handle. When life seems impossible, what do you do? Who do you turn to for help?

10. Clay was mad at his dad for not getting him out of trouble when he was arrested. He had to do community service and he thought Daniel should have made it all go away. Have you dealt with a child or person who felt that way? How did you handle it? Did he face his consequences?

11. Who do you think killed Uncle Tyler and Axle? Why?

12. Melora's housekeeper, Juanita, who she considered a friend, too, was spying on Melora

for Uncle Tyler. Have you had a friend betray you like that? What did you do? Did you ever forgive the friend?

13. The Alamo Planning Committee wouldn't give in to the threats implied about the upcoming celebration and change the plans for it. Do you think that was the right decision? Why or why not?

14. Melora was scared of her husband. He used threats to keep her with him. Have you ever been in a situation like that? What did you do to form a healthier relationship?

15. What were some things that made Melora fall in love with Daniel? What were some things that made Daniel fall in love with Melora?

LARGER-PRINT BOOKS!

**GET 2 FREE
LARGER-PRINT NOVELS
PLUS 2 FREE
MYSTERY GIFTS**

Love Inspired®
SUSPENSE
RIVETING INSPIRATIONAL ROMANCE

Larger-print novels are now available...

YES! Please send me 2 FREE LARGER-PRINT Love Inspired® Suspense novels and my 2 FREE mystery gifts (gifts are worth about $10). After receiving them, if I don't wish to receive any more books, I can return the shipping statement marked "cancel". If I don't cancel, I will receive 4 brand-new novels every month and be billed just $4.74 per book in the U.S. or $5.24 per book in Canada. That's a saving of at least 24% off the cover price. It's quite a bargain! Shipping and handling is just 50¢ per book in the U.S. and 75¢ per book in Canada.* I understand that accepting the 2 free books and gifts places me under no obligation to buy anything. I can always return a shipment and cancel at any time. Even if I never buy another book, the two free books and gifts are mine to keep forever.

110/310 IDN FC7L

Name	(PLEASE PRINT)

Address	Apt. #

City	State/Prov.	Zip/Postal Code

Signature (if under 18, a parent or guardian must sign)

Mail to the **Reader Service:**
IN U.S.A.: P.O. Box 1867, Buffalo, NY 14240-1867
IN CANADA: P.O. Box 609, Fort Erie, Ontario L2A 5X3

Not valid for current subscribers to Love Inspired Suspense larger-print books.

**Are you a current subscriber to Love Inspired Suspense books
and want to receive the larger-print edition?
Call 1-800-873-8635 or visit www.ReaderService.com.**

* Terms and prices subject to change without notice. Prices do not include applicable taxes. Sales tax applicable in N.Y. Canadian residents will be charged applicable taxes. Offer not valid in Quebec. This offer is limited to one order per household. All orders subject to credit approval. Credit or debit balances in a customer's account(s) may be offset by any other outstanding balance owed by or to the customer. Please allow 4 to 6 weeks for delivery. Offer available while quantities last.

Your Privacy—The Reader Service is committed to protecting your privacy. Our Privacy Policy is available online at www.ReaderService.com or upon request from the Reader Service.

We make a portion of our mailing list available to reputable third parties that offer products we believe may interest you. If you prefer that we not exchange your name with third parties, or if you wish to clarify or modify your communication preferences, please visit us at www.ReaderService.com/consumerschoice or write to us at Reader Service Preference Service, P.O. Box 9062, Buffalo, NY 14269. Include your complete name and address.